ALL BLEEDING STOPS EVENTUALLY

A Lenny Moss Mystery

By Timothy Sheard

HARDBALL

PRESS

THE REVIEWERS PRAISE LENNY MOSS!

This Won't Hurt A Bit

"...when a troublesome laundry worker is charged with the [medical intern's] murder, outraged staff members go to their union representative, a scrappy custodian named Lenny Moss, and ask him to find the real killer. Since there's no merit to the case against the laundry worker to begin with, Lenny is just wasting his time. But Sheard ...makes sure that readers do not waste theirs. His intimate view of Lenny's world is a gentle eyeopener into the way a large institution looks from a workingman's perspective." ~**New York Times**

Some Cuts Never Heal

"This well-plotted page-turner is guaranteed to scare the bejesus out of anyone anticipating a hospital stay anytime in the near future." ~**Publishers Weekly**

"Sheard provides...polished prose and elements of warmth and humor. Strongly recommended for most mystery collections."
~**Library Journal**

A Race Against Death

"While most shop stewards do not get involved in murder mysteries, they solve tough problems at work every day. Now they can look up to a fictional role model—Super Steward Lenny Moss." ~**Public Employee Press**

"Timothy Sheard provides a delightful hospital investigative tale that grips readers from the moment that Dr. Singh and his team apply CPR, but fail." ~**Mysteries Galore**

Slim To None

"Here's a great read, a complicated mystery, good friends, comradeship in hard times, and union workers shown in full humanity." ~**AFSCME 3506**

"Laced with dark humor and told with an insider's knowledge, this fast-paced, nifty paperback is the best yet in the series."
~**Curious Book Reviews**

A Bitter Pill

"*A Bitter Pill* ... is a short, fast, tight book, giving us what we like best about Lenny Moss, hospital custodian and union steward." ~**WORKING USA**

No Place To Be Sick

"Does such a wonderful job of showing workers uniting to fight for justice that...unions have used Sheard's books for steward training. Find out if Lenny & his friends win their battle in this roller coaster of a story." **Union Communications**

"There's enough suspense, fear and chills running up and down your spine to make you keep on reading it in one fell swoop. Watch your back if you're alone in the house!"

~Pride & A Paycheck

Someone Has To Die

"The setting, characters and dialogue are so realistic, you feel as though you have walked down the halls of James Madison Hospital and met the folks who work there... This is a book about working people who...draw deep down on a reserve of strength and intelligence that enables them to stay afloat amidst a rising tide of social and economic waves of adversity."
~Labor Press

"Lenny does it again! Another corpse. Another murderer. Another management's cruel calamity of ignorance. But this time, add some incredible union organizing to cheer about. Then give Brother Moss and his friends a shot of decent bourbon for keeping us on the edge of a certain hospital death bed."
~Pride & A Paycheck

One Foot in the Grave

"Sheard...seasons the plot with union wisdom and principled action designed to build workers' power on the job... You don't have to be a union member to enjoy the ride, but activists will get a special kick from Lenny Moss and his stalwart co-workers." **~PhillyLabor.com**

"This gripping mystery story is overlaid with a rich description of work life in the James Madison Hospital...Reading the latest Lenny Moss novel, really all of them, will entertain, educate, and inspire. **~Portside**

Published by Hard Ball Press.

Information available at: www.hardballpress.com

ISBN: 978-1-7344938-0-1

Cover art by Patty Henderson

www.boulevardphotografica.yolasite.com.

Exterior and interior book design by D. Bass

Library of Congress Cataloging-in-Publication Data

Sheard, Timothy

All Bleeding Stops Eventually: A Lenny Moss Mystery/Timothy Sheard

1. Philadelphia (PA) 2. Hospitals. 3. Lenny Moss. 4. Labor union

DEDICATION

This book is lovingly dedicated to my union brothers and sisters around the world, and to the workers who yearn for union representation but have yet to win the battle.

"They say barbed wire fences make good neighbors."

Chris Sheard, *Their Lips Are Moving But Got Nothing to Say*

On Monday morning at 6:15 AM, Clair Bowen stumbled and almost fell as she walked up the ramp to the James Madison Hospital Emergency Department. Stepping inside, she approached the window of the intake clerk and tapped on the glass. The clerk looked up from her computer, saw an attractive young woman with straggly, long blonde hair, loose clothes and a furrowed brow.

"Yes, may I help you?" said the clerk, offering a friendly smile.

"I'm sick. I think I'm bleeding. My stools are black and I have this terrible pain in my abdomen and I can't hold down my food..."

"Take the blue form from the rack on the wall, it's right over there, fill it out and drop it in the slot, someone will be with your shortly. Okay, sweetie?"

"Yes, but I really can't wait. I...I think I'm going to—"

Suddenly Clair's mouth opened and a stream of dark blood poured forth. The blood ran down her shirt and onto the floor. She began to sway from side to side, threatening to collapse.

"Oh Jesus," said the clerk. "Don't faint! Don't faint, please lady, stay on your feet, I'll get someone to help you!"

The clerk jumped up from her seat and hurried back to the bays, where nurses, doctors and techs were already busy with a full room of stricken patients. "I've got a GI bleeder in the lobby! She looks like she's about to pass out!"

A burly tech who had just drawn blood from an elderly man zipped up the plastic bag with the vials of blood and dropped it into the Out basket. "I'll get her," he said. The tech grabbed a wheelchair, spun it around and punched the metal plate on the wall. As the double doors slowly swung open, he rushed through to the lobby.

Clair was leaning against a wall, trying to hold back the vomiting. She wiped her chin with her sleeve. "I'm sorry to make a mess," she said in a weak voice. "I'm so sorry."

"It's okay, miss, we see that all the time. Just settle into the chair and I'll bring you back." The tech turned the chair and pushed it back through the open doors. "My name's Kevin. Everyone calls me Kev. We'll get you on a stretcher and the doctor will check you out lickety-split. All right?"

Clair nodded her head. "I'm so weak and dizzy."

Kev helped Clair stand up and settle onto a stretcher in the one empty bay. After first assessing her blood pressure and pulse to be sure she wasn't in shock, the ER tech handed her a hospital gown and promised to return with a wash basin so she could clean herself up before changing into the gown. "Just toss your clothes in this plastic bag, you can send it home to be laundered later." He drew the curtain closed, then fetched a basin of water, towel and washrag. He set the basin on an overbed table and handed her the towel and washrag. "Doctor Stone will see you in a sec. Don't worry, he's the best, you'll be okay. Really, you will."

Clair mouthed a thank you and began to pull off her sweater. She folded it neatly and tucked it in the plastic bag, then she removed her bra and began washing her face and neck. It was all so overwhelming. And frightening. She shivered as she ran the wet washrag over her chest, raising goosebumps and making her wonder if she would ever feel warm again.

<>

After waiting for what seemed like an hour but was only a few minutes, Clair heard a gentle male voice outside the curtain say, "Are you dressed, miss? May I come in?"

"I'm okay, yes," said Clair.

Dr. Robert Stone parted the curtains and stepped in, followed by Kevin. Stone was a tall, red-haired man with a boyish face and a warm smile. He wore pink scrubs and white clogs. "Hello," he said. "I'm Doctor Stone. I'm the physician in charge of your care."

"Pleased to meet you. I'm Clair. Clair Bowen."

"I'm happy to meet you, Clair. This must seem like a scary place to you, but we're going to take the best care of you that we can. Kev is going to draw a little blood, not enough to bother you, so we can see what's what, and then he'll give you a nice sterile intravenous solution with a bit of minerals. That will get you feeling a whole lot better in no time. And while he's doing that, the clerk will take your information and plug you into the system. All right?"

As the tech fastened an elastic tourniquet around her arm and set out his blood drawing equipment, Dr. Stone asked the patient when did she first notice signs of bleeding. She told him it had started about a week ago. At first she only noticed her stool was getting darker and darker, and she had terrible abdominal cramps, mostly after eating. This morning she threw up blood.

The physician lifted her gown and listened to her bowel sounds with his stethoscope. Then he gently pressed on Clair's belly. "Is this painful? I'm sorry, I have to press a little bit."

Clair winced when he pressed on her lower abdomen. "I could only drink a cup of tea this morning, nothing else would stay down."

Stone continued his physical exam, asking more of her history: did she have any chronic medical conditions? "No." Had she ever been told she had trouble with her blood clotting? "No." Had she been taking aspirin on a regular basis?

"Yes, I have been taking aspirin for maybe a month. I fell and banged my knee on a cement step. It was extremely painful, so I took aspirin for the pain."

"What did the x-ray show?" asked Stone.

3

"Oh, I didn't get an x-ray. I never went to a doctor, I just hobbled around for a few weeks. It's a lot better, really it is, but it still hurts if I try to kneel or carry any weight."

"Well we're going to watch you and monitor your bleeding, and if the bleeding doesn't stop, we'll have to look at your esophagus and stomach with a scope. But for now, we'll just watch and wait and hope for the best."

Instructing Clair to settle back on the stretcher and let Kevin insert the IV catheter and begin infusing the intravenous fluids, Stone stepped out of the bay, took a dollop of alcohol gel from a wall dispenser and rubbed it into his hands and wrists, then he entered a quick note in her electronic chart. As he was finishing the note, the clerk asked if this was going to be a critical care admission. Stone told her he needed to see the lab results and follow her vital signs. If she was stable she could go to a ward.

Stone suspected that the chronic aspirin ingestion had irritated the lining of her stomach. At the same time, the aspirin had impaired the patient's ability to form blood clots. It had "greased the platelets" as the medical staff liked to describe it colloquially. That anti-coagulant effect led the stomach ulcer to open the flood gates and bleed out.

He hoped it wasn't a case of esophageal varices, ligating swollen veins in the esophagus was a risky procedure. He didn't like to think about the mortality rate of a variceal bleed in the presence of an anti-coagulated blood stream. It was high. Too high for a nice young woman with her whole life ahead of her.

He was a man of modest proportions. Not very tall, with a large nose, thick black eyebrows and a bald spot on the back of his head that his wife swore was getting larger every day. His dark eyes suffered no fools. Though his hands were rough and calloused from years of manual labor, his touch could be gentle, almost delicate.

As Lenny Moss poured a cup of bleach in the stainless steel bucket, Mimi Rogers, one of the nurses on the day shift, stopped at the housekeeping closet. "I'm so glad they let you use that bleach on the floors, Lenny," she said. "I love the way it smells."

"Yeah, it does tickle the nose, doesn't it? Reminds me of going swimming in the city pool when I was a kid." He plunged his mop into the soapy water and wheeled the bucket out onto the Seven South ward. "Ready for another day in paradise?"

"Oh, yes, everything is just hunky-dory," the nurse replied in a sing-song voice. "I just love working at James Madison Hospital! James Madison is the *best* hospital in all of Philadelphia!"

Mimi finished her remarks by opening her mouth and pantomiming sticking her fingers down her throat and vomiting. Lenny did his best to control a laugh, knowing that the hospital dispatcher could hear every word that Mimi spoke, since the nurses were forced to wear the hated GPS unit around their neck while on duty. They weren't even allowed to turn it off when they were in the bathroom, leading the nurses to believe the dispatcher could hear if they were doing "Number One or Number Two."

As the nurse went on to the station to take morning report, Lenny began mopping the floor, which was streaked with long black marks from the soiled wheels of a stretcher or wheelchair. He set out the yellow CAUTION – WET FLOOR sign to mark off the wet section of floor. With the pungent odor of bleach tickling his nose, he dropped the mop in the bucket and took a minute to plan out his day.

All week long the housekeeping supervisor had pulled his partner Little Mary to Seven-North, leaving him alone on the South ward to empty all the trash receptacles, mop all the floors and clean up all the spills that patients and staff inevitably left behind them, not to mention cleaning all the discharge rooms. The hospital administration was hell bent on maximizing their income stream, so empty beds were not allowed to stay empty long.

Noting a sticky dark mass on the floor that his mop hadn't picked up, he pulled the wide putty knife from his belt and ran the blade under the mass. It came loose easily, meaning it was fresh. He dropped it into a nearby trash bucket with a sigh, wondering, as he had for too many years, why he didn't go into some easier line of work. Like commercial fishing. In the Arctic Ocean off the coast of Alaska.

Lenny spied a familiar figure walking toward him: a stout woman with short cropped bronze colored hair and a tattoo of a morning dove on her arm. Margie Aquinos, one of the housekeepers on the midnight shift, shouted to Lenny even before she reached him. "He's screwing me up the ass, Lenny! You've gotta help me! I can't take this shit. Swear to god, I'm gonna kill somebody if you don't help me!"

"Margie, calm down, please. Take a deep breath, exhale and tell me what's the problem."

A moment of silence. "Okay, sorry, it's just that bastard supervisor Nasir has got me so fricking upset. When I came off duty this morning I found a letter in my slot at the timeclock. It was about my request for paid maternity leave. You remember, Sissy had a baby girl."

"Of course, we took up a collection for you in Housekeeping, I was glad we could help you guys out."

"Yeah, it was great, thanks. Really helped a lot. So anyway, I put in my request for the leave, and I figure everything is hunky dory, and then when I went to punch out this morning fricking Neo-Nazi Nasir leaves me this letter saying that James Madison does not offer *paid leave* to... wait a second, I'll read it to you. Does not 'provide compensated leave time for women who are not the biological mother to the child.' Do you *believe* this shit?"

"I can believe anything coming out of Croesus. Ever since that scumbag hedge fund bought James Madison and took it private they've been digging away at cutting costs and finding new ways to make a profit. Your being only the wife of the mother gives them an excuse to deny you your paid leave. Unpaid leave they can't deny you, it's the law, but they don't have to pay your salary."

"They can't get away with this shit, can they, Lenny? Tell me they can't deny me my benefits."

"I'll call the union lawyer. We'll file a grievance and push it as far as we have to. It's discrimination against you for your lifestyle, plus, it's just wrong. Oh, and you should know the union's got another case with the same issue, a guy in billing, so I'm gonna push for making this a class action grievance. Go home and get some sleep, I'll let you know what the union says about the case."

"They damn well better give me my pay. If they don't somebody's gonna regret it!"

Watching Margie walk away, Lenny understood Margie's anger all too well. He recalled how when Croesus first took over James Madison Hospital, they tried to decertify the union, arguing that their corporate office had not signed the original union contract and was under no obligation to honor it now. Only militant union action inside the hospital coupled with organized support from the community convinced Croesus to honor the contract and negotiate a renewal. Margie had been in the protest outside the facility every day, sometimes leading chants and always ready for a fight.

The following year the administration threatened to withdraw from the health and safety fund, which would make the union benefits fund insolvent. Hundreds of retirees would lose their health benefits, a death sentence for many of them. Once again, the HSWU rallied community support all the way to the capitol in Harrisburg, and the hospital agreed to continue paying their share into the fund.

He cursed softly under his breath, glad that the housekeepers were not required to wear the hated GPS units around their necks, so the dispatcher couldn't hear him.

"Sons of bitches," he said aloud, raising a smile on Celeste's lips.

"They never give up finding ways to screw us, do they, Lenny?" said the Seven South ward clerk.

"Never."

"You figure out what you're gonna give Patience for her birthday?" asked Celeste. Celeste always looked good. Today she was decked out in a colorful brown and gold tunic, a copper necklace and copper earrings. Patience had often pointed out the clerk's jewelry and clothing, it was her way of hinting at what she wanted him to get her for a birthday or Christmas. When he was in a store, Lenny had taken to snapping pictures of the item he was considering and sending them to Celeste for her opinion. So far, he was batting 500 with his gifts, a big improvement over previous years.

"No, I don't know what I'm gonna get her, but I've still got some time."

"A week, you call that time?"

"Hey, gimme a break, I've been busy!"

Celeste laughed. She knew Lenny had been busy, with workers constantly coming to him with problems, many of them with issues that were outside the contract, like immigration problems or money worries. Lenny always found time to help them. "Well if you want me to go shopping for you, let me know."

Lenny thanked her and promised to send photos for approval when he was in the store. With a sigh he went to the housekeeping locker to dig up a grievance form, he wanted to file the papers by the end of his shift. But first he would use his lunch hour to interview the other aggrieved worker who was also being denied paid parental leave.

"Emergency Nurse on line two for Nurse Rogers!" The dispatcher's voice blared from the GPS unit hanging around Mimi's neck, cutting Mimi off in mid-sentence. Irritated at yet another intrusion into her day, Mimi hurried to the nursing station to take the report. The ER Nurse summarized the case, describing the dark red blood the woman had vomited up, her dark stool and her complaints of dizziness and abdominal pain.

The ER nurse added, "Miss Bowen reports taking aspirin on a daily basis for several weeks. Doctor Stone believes that was a big factor in the bleeding." When Mimi asked why the patient wasn't being admitted to the intensive care unit, which was the usual practice for an active GI bleed, the ER nurse admitted that the lab report was puzzling. "Her admitting hemoglobin and hematocrit were normal. That surprised Doctor Stone, but at first he put it down to volume contraction in her blood stream."

"She got IV hydration, didn't she?" said Mimi.

"Of course. But the repeat H&H was not that much lower, plus her vital signs were always in the normal range. So now the doctor thinks it was a nose bleed that she swallowed, you know how dramatic they can be."

Mimi thanked the ER nurse and told her they could send the patient up, the bed was ready. Then she asked Rose, the nurse's aide working with her, to be sure to have an emesis basis and extra towels at the bedside, those GI bleeders always left a trail of bloody stool behind them.

<>

Twenty minutes after taking report from the ER nurse, Mimi greeted Clair Bowen as the transporter pushed the wheelchair into the room. After transferring the IV bag to a pole at the head of the bed, the nurse grasped the patient's upper arm and gently guided her up out of the chair and onto the bed. Then the nurse grasped the top sheet and bedspread, which had been folded like a fan at the foot of the bed, and covered the woman up to her chest.

"Let me show you the bed controls," Mimi said, pointing to the buttons imbedded in the side rail.

"That's okay, I know how to use them," said Clair.

"Oh, have you been in a hospital before?"

"Uh, no, but I've visited a friend a couple of times." She pressed the button and raised the head of the bed, then she turned on the overbed light.

Mimi went through the normal admitting procedure, taking vital signs, filling in a form with a lot of questions and checking the doctor's admission orders. The nurse was relieved that the patient's blood count was in the normal range, so she wouldn't be administering a blood transfusion, which always carried a risk of a reaction, no matter how carefully the lab matched the patient to the donor.

"You can have clear liquids for lunch, do you think you can hold something down?"

Clair shrugged. "I don't know, I'm afraid of throwing up again. I don't want to make a mess of your nice clean sheets."

"Oh, don't worry about them, our laundry handles all kinds of nasty stuff." She placed a kidney-shaped emesis basis on the overbed table. "Just use this if you have to, and don't worry about a mess, we're used to it."

Finished with her interview, Mimi reminded her patient to use the intercom to let the dispatcher know if she needed anything. "I'll hear that bad boy on this device, so you won't have to wait long to see me," she said, lifting the GPS unit from her chest. "Okay?"

"Okay. I'll try not to bother you."

"Bother me all you want!"

Clair sniffed the air. "Do I smell bleach?"

"Yes, housekeeping uses it to kill the germs. Is it bothering you? The smell will be gone in a few minutes."

"No, I like the smell, it feels clean. Thank you." Clair pulled the sheet up to her chin and closed her eyes. "I think I'll just rest a while."

"Good. I'll bring you lunch in an hour so." Mimi hurried off. She didn't dare get behind schedule administering medications to her patients, the computer recorded the time of every drug administration. If she was more than 15 minutes late, the system put up a red flag and the nurse had to explain to her head nurse why she had been "late" with the medication. Again.

<>

Regis Devoe set out the instruments for the autopsy: the small circular saw for cutting through the skull, the breastbone, ribs. The knives, pliers and large syringes for aspirating fluid from the chest and peritoneal cavity, and specimen cups of varying sizes for specimens to go to the pathology lab. The strong overhead fluorescent light glinted on the stainless steel table, with its troughs for collecting blood and other fluids and the hose for washing it all down the drain.

Whistling a syncopated tune, he marveled at how good his life was going. It was a surprise, even to him: Doctor Fingers, the chief pathologist, had urged him to sign up for the two-year associate program for pathology technician. The doctor had even offered to pay the tuition from a fund the hospital had, though Regis suspected that the "fund" had really just been the good doctor's own money.

Regis hadn't been sure he could handle the classes, but his wife Serena pushed him. Even though he had serious doubts he could pass the tests, Regis had agreed, and damn if the study material was drop dead interesting. Having assisted in the morgue for two years, he already had a good handle on the anatomy and physiology, and the microbiology hadn't been half as tough as he had feared.

He was a long way from the days working in the laundry, when he was getting written up all the time for coming in late or for talking back to a boss or a security guard. He sure had kept Lenny busy defending him. But now, all in all, life was good.

Probably it wouldn't last forever, shit always ended up stinking up the soles of your shoes eventually. For now he was riding the wave of good fortune and looking forward to the raise in pay when he finished the program.

"Morning, Regis," said Dr. Fingers, looking in to the autopsy suite. "All set for a case?"

"All set, doc. What is it you like to say? Everything 'ship shape and Bristol fashion?'"

"That's it."

"I don't know what it means, but I think I've got you covered."

"You can pull the Mulvey body from the box, we'll start in an hour."

Regis made his way down the hall to the large walk-in cold storage locker where they kept the bodies waiting for autopsy or to be taken away by the undertaker. He found the body, double-checked the name and ID number on the toe tag, and dragged the body onto the stretcher, noting, as he often had, that the term "stiff" was really not the right term for the corpses. Once rigor mortis passed, the body was remarkably flexible. He wheeled the stretcher with the Mulvey body out of the box, again whistling a syncopated rhythm as he walked.

<>

14

Sitting in the ER break room, Doctor Stone closed his eyes and sniffed the herbal tea in his cupped hands. His wife Maribella had encouraged him to switch to the herbal brew, saying, "You have so much energy, Bobby, you don't *need* caffeine in your system. You get your adrenalin rush from the patients already!"

He opened his eyes, took a long sip and smiled, thinking about his wife. He recalled their early courtship days, when after they both finished their shift in the ER — she worked with him as a nurse at the time — she'd climbed on the back of his Harley motorcycle, wrapped her arms around him and they'd ridden all over the Delaware Valley. Maribella complained at first about having to wear a helmet, she wanted to feel the wind in her hair, it was long and dark and sexy. But she agreed to wear it in the end. Stone had seen far too fractured skulls of motorcyclists who hadn't worn their helmet to take no for an answer.

Now she was home with their second child, a plump little nine-month old boy who was learning to stand while holding onto a table or chair. Sometimes he would let go and fall back, but the diaper cushioned his fall, so he smiled instead of crying. Stone smiled at the memory of his children and wife, then his smile faded. He pondered the case of Clair Bowen. How could she produce dark red blood from the mouth and still have a normal hemoglobin? Maybe the normal lab result was just volume contraction. Maybe the blood was from a simple nose bleed, not a GI source, nose bleeds could produce prodigious amounts of blood from the mouth.

Stone didn't like the nose bleed diagnosis, given the patient's report of abdominal pain and dizziness. There was something else going on. Something out of the ordinary. It was a puzzle, especially the normal hemoglobin and hematocrit, and he wasn't going to let a puzzle go unsolved, even if the patient was no longer in the ER.

What was it his good friend Michael Auginello in Infectious Disease liked to say, referencing a Monty Python movie? "When you hear the sound of hoofbeats, don't always think of coconuts."

Or horses. Think outside the most likely diagnosis. Imagine the unexpected.

In other words, prepare for the worst.

4

Picking up a sandwich and a large coffee in the cafeteria for his lunch, Lenny hurried to the hospital billing department. He had just enough time to go over the issue with the co-worker, eat the sandwich and gulp down the coffee...unless somebody *else* called him with a problem.

He passed Hilda, who waved at him from her cubby where she was on the phone with somebody about their hospital bill, and looked in the section where Woodrow Theodore Wilson worked.

"Hey, Woody, this a good time?"

Woody looked up from a pile of papers scattered across his desk. It looked as if a sudden wind had stirred up the stacks of folders, but Lenny suspected that the man really did know where all of them belonged. Woody was dressed in a pale blue button-down shirt, dark blue bow tie with polka dots, khaki-colored chinos and loafers.

"Hello, Lenny. No, it's not a good time, but it's *never* a good time around here, you know that." Woody swiveled around in his chair and reached out a hand. "Thanks for taking my case. I wouldn't trust it with anyone but you."

"Flattery will get you very far with me. Just don't forget I'm a happily married man."

"The best ones are always taken." Woody showed a hangdog expression, then an impish smile. "I'm not your type anyway, Lenny, I'm a guy."

"And a great guy if I may say so. But tell me what's going on."

"Jesus give me strength. I put in my request for paid paternity leave, just like anybody else. Just like, you know..."

"Any straight father would do."

"Ex-actly. I put in my papers, along with a copy of our boy's birth certificate. I even included photos of the little tyke, which you really don't have to do, it's not required or anything, and the bastards said I wasn't entitled to the leave because *A*, I'm not the bio-logical father, and *B*, I'm not the 'wife'. I mean, what the fuck, Lenny, are they *kidding* me?"

"I know, Woody, it's legal bullshit, Croesus is riding the wave of anti-LGBT laws. They'll do anything to cut our benefits, you know the drill."

"Do I ever. This administration is so damn *greedy*. It breaks my heart whenever I send out a past due notice. Did you know Legal has been suing patients for unpaid bills? Suing *poor people!* Why would they do that?"

Lenny explained that ever since Croesus had bought out James Madison, they were trying to change their patient demographics to attract more upscale patients. That was why they remodeled the 8th floor and put in executive suites, complete with maid service. The word goes around the working class communities, if you don't have the bucks for the co-pay, go to Temple. "It's a slick strategy," Lenny added, "and it's perfectly legal."

Woody asked if the union couldn't do something about the lawsuits against the poor patients. Lenny said he would bring up the issue at their next delegates meeting, the union had a long history of supporting community issues, like immigrant rights and gentrification, and Lenny had been on the front lines for a long time. When the police fire-bombed the house of a radical back-to-the-land black commune, killing eleven people, parents and children, the union had called for justice. Lenny had been arrested in the first of the many protest marches against the police, and the union had vigorously supported the campaign for justice.

He told Woody about Margie's case and his plan to file a class action grievance. Woody thought that was a great idea that would strengthen both of the cases.

"I'll file the grievance today and contact the union. Their labor lawyer will look over the contract and the hospital bylaws and tell us what our chances are."

Woody shook Lenny's hand again and thanked him profusely. "You can't imagine the weight you've lifted off of my shoulders. Just knowing that the union's on my side means so much. I understand we could still lose the case, but at least we're standing up to these cruel, sadistic people. Who run a god damn hospital!"

<>

When the lunch trays were passed out, Mimi went in to check on Clair and saw the young woman had not touched her clear liquid diet. "What, no appetite? You know there's always room for Jello."

Clair told the nurse she wasn't hungry. Mimi asked how she liked her tea and added milk and sugar. Setting the cup in front of Clair, the nurse asked her to try and take in a little nourishment. "You can't rely on that IV fluid to meet your needs, you have to eat something. Try a little broth, okay?"

Clair promised to try. She pulled the lid off the bowl of soup, sniffed it and made a face. "It smells awful." Mimi confessed it wasn't exactly homemade. With a heavy sigh, Clare reached for the Jello and plunged a spoon into the quivering green mass. As she took a small bite from the spoon, Mimi thanked her and hurried off to give out her twelve o'clock meds.

After the noon meds were given out and the lunch trays collected, Rose, the nurse's aide, asked Mimi if Clair had bathroom privileges. The nurse told her the patient could walk to the bathroom as long as she wasn't dizzy getting up. "Tell her to hold onto the rolling IV pole, that will steady her, but stay with her, okay, Rose?"

19

The aide promised to stay with the patient. Twenty minutes later Rose reported that Clair had walked to the bathroom and back without feeling dizzy. She'd even finished all of her Jello and tea.

Mimi was relieved. She was also thankful that there had been no further episodes of active bleeding. She hoped the bleeding had stopped and there would be no emergency surgery or other risky procedure.

Rose added, "Oh, Mimi, Miss Bowen asked me to draw the curtain across her bed, so I did, is that okay? It means you won't be able to see her from the doorway."

"Well...normally I like to see my patients as I make my rounds. But she's not unstable, her H&H is still normal. I guess we can respect her privacy this one time. But do look in through the curtains from time to time, okay?"

Rose promised to be vigilant. As the aide went on to collect the lunch trays, Mimi wondered if Clair had serious self-esteem issues: was she ashamed of her body or embarrassed that a man might see her dressed only in a hospital gown? Mimi made a mental note to gently ask the patient about her fears once they'd gotten to know each other better. For now, Mimi let the matter rest, planning to bring the topic up the next morning when she came back on duty and the patient had become more comfortable in the hospital setting.

<>

The autopsy completed, Regis placed the specimen containers in a cart for delivery to the requisite labs. Before leaving the autopsy suite, he transferred the body to a stretcher. He thought the cadaver, now neatly sewed back together, looked better than before entering the department, and understood that a little bit of cosmetic work was an important part of the pathologist's duties. They needed to always consider that the family will view the body at the wake.

Regis wheeled the stretcher down the hall to the cold locker and transferred the body to a table in a space toward the back. Closing the heavy door, he remembered the time that a real nasty bastard had locked Lenny in the cold storage locker. Nobody had heard his cries for help, and Lenny would have frozen to death if Moose hadn't gone searching for him. Ever since then, the staff had removed the lock on the big door and made sure nobody living could ever be imprisoned in that grisly place again.

5

At three o'clock, Lenny hung up his mop head, rinsed the bucket and set the housekeeping locker in order. Then he called his wife Patience and told her he'd be a few minutes late getting off work, he had to file a grievance with Human Resources. With Patience agreeing to meet him in the employee parking lot, he went to the housekeeping locker room in the basement, where he retrieved a grievance form. It was a thick form, with old-fashioned carbon between the sheets to make copies. Lenny always marveled how his union stuck with old school technologies.

Sitting on the long bench in the locker room, Lenny carefully described the nature of the grievance, citing city and state regulations that prohibited discriminating against workers on the basis of sexual orientation or gender. Then he placed the completed form in an envelope that had the union logo on the front.

He punched out at the timeclock, chuckling, as he did on many an afternoon as he recalled the time Regis Devoe had poured Krazy Glue into the slot where the workers inserted their cards. It was a protest against the draconian rules that allowed the bosses to dock workers, and even suspend them, if they were more than seven minutes late to punch in. Seven minutes!

With the timeclock disabled, Supervisor Childress had been forced to go back to an old paper ledger, getting the workers to sign in and out until the department replaced the clock, which had been permanently destroyed. A small victory often celebrated over the years with a drink and a lusty toast.

Lenny trod down the thickly carpeted hallway of the executive suite to Human Resources. He entered without a knock — it wasn't as if they could keep him out — and approached Miss Sneet, the office manager. Sneet was a humorless woman always dressed in gray or black. She never wore lipstick, perhaps, Lenny speculated, because her lips were so thin they afforded no surface for applying the color. But then, he couldn't imagine anyone wanting to kiss her, anyway.

"I've here to file a grievance," Lenny said, standing in front of her desk.

"What is it this time, Mister Moss? You have your precious bleach solution."

"It's a little more involved than that." He pulled the form from the union envelope and handed it to her. The manager held it at arm's length as if it might be contaminated with some antibiotic-resistant germ and moved her thin lips as she read the statement. Without a trace of humor, she said, "I will leave this for Mister Freely, he is in a meeting at the moment."

"That's fine, but I still need you to time stamp it and give me the back copy."

Sneet glared at him. She resented when Lenny held her to the letter of the contract, especially when it was to prevent her from pulling some cheap legal trick. Management was known to claim that a grievance was invalid because it had supposedly been filed more than 30 days from the alleged incidence. as the union contract required. Lenny *always* insisted the recipient stamp the time for his records, just to be safe.

She shoved the form into her machine, which printed the date and time with a loud CLACK! Then she tore off the back copy and handed it to him without a word and without looking up at him.

Lenny turned and left without saying good-bye. He knew when he wasn't wanted.

Out in the employee parking lot, he saw Patience chatting with Sandy, one of the old security guards. The man had thick jowls that jiggled when he talked, a deep voice and an easy smile. Whenever Lenny asked Sandy why he didn't retire, the man was old enough and had enough time on the job, Sandy would grin and say, "What, sit at home all day and look at the wife? I've seen enough of her these fifty years."

"Yo, Lenny," Sandy called. "I see you finally gave up that old Buick of yours. It was running kinda rough and putting out some smoke, but did you have to get something so small? Seems like a stiff wind would just blow this car off the road."

"Har, har. We wanted something easy on the gas, and this one goes like a hundred miles on a gallon. It's got a big rubber band for going uphill."

"I like our Echo just fine," said Patience, getting into the passenger seat. "It's just my size. I think it's cute."

On the drive home, Lenny told his wife about the class action grievance he'd filed and how Miss Sneet had practically bit his hand when he insisted that she stamp it for time and date. Patience shook her head, forever amazed at the low tactics the bosses tried to use.

When they reached the house, they found Malcolm and Takia were home from school. Malcolm was watching cartoons on the TV in the living, but he turned off the set as soon as he heard his parents at the front door.

"Mommy, can I play football at school? The coach said I'm a natural, he saw me on the playground. I threw the ball a thousand miles, it was awesome!"

"No, you are not playing football, you're eight years old, it's too dangerous, you could suffer a concussion. The game should be banned from school, anyway."

Malcolm stuck out his lower lip and looked to Lenny for support. But Lenny knew better than to contradict Patience in front of the children. They'd had many an argument when he first married her and became a stepfather to Malcolm and Takia, the boy's older sister, but always in private, and always with quiet voices.

"Your mom and I'll talk about it," he told Malcolm. "But don't get your hopes up, your mother is right, the game can give you serious injuries. She knows, she's seen the x-rays."

"Homework, now!" Patience said, pointing to her son's backpack.

"Oh-kay," said Malcolm, hanging his head in sorrow. "But Lenny got to help me, the word jumble is impossible!"

"Lenny *has got* to help you," she corrected him. "I don't want to hear any of that street language in my house. Understand?"

"Yes, ma'am." Malcolm took his workbook out of the bag and pushed it at Lenny's chest, then he trudged upstairs.

While Patience thawed some roast beef in the kitchen for dinner, Lenny called the union hall and asked for the area rep who covered James Madison. That took him to voicemail, so he left a brief message explaining about the class action grievance he'd filed and that he would email a copy once he'd had a chance to scan it on his computer.

Hanging up, he sent a text message to Dave Rambler, one of the union lawyers, saying they needed to talk about an LGBT discrimination grievance. Rambler had defended Lenny in the past, along with several of his co-workers, when they had occupied the office of the hospital President. The lawyer been a solid supporter of the militant tactics, and a good friend ever since.

Satisfied he had done all he could for the night, Lenny poured two fingers of Evan Williams bourbon in a glass, added some ice and went to the stairs. As he started up the stairs, Patience called out to him, "You're setting a terrible example, helping Malcolm with his homework while drinking whiskey!"

Lenny called back that was exactly the point, the child needed to learn what real men drank, and that when work left you tired and fed up, the only salvation was in the bottle.

6

At 7:30 PM, Mimi greeted the night nurse Catherine with a look of relief. Having completed her third twelve-hour shift in a row, Mimi was worn out and ready for a long break. Her feet hurt, her back ached and she needed a long soak in a hot tub with a glass of icy cold beer and her husband Louis massaging her tired shoulders.

It was always a comfort giving Catherine report, there was no better nurse on the graveyard shift. Mimi had been worried when her friend delivered her baby in the middle of that terrible, hot summer. Lilly had been premature and the birth had occurred during the height of the Zika outbreak. The virulent new strain of the virus had pregnant mothers scared to go outside least they be bitten by an infected mosquito.

Catherine had been terrified her child would be born with brain abnormalities because she had suffered a host of mosquito bites while walking their dog. But in the end the baby was fine and soon overcame the problems of her premature birth.

When Mimi reported on Clair, the GI bleed, she told Catherine how the patient's H&H had been stable. "Doctor Stone thought she might have a nose bleed and not an actual GI bleed, that's why he didn't admit her to the ICU. She'll need another blood draw at midnight." Catherine made a note on her report sheet and drew a square around the midnight lab request as a reminder to check the STAT results. If it came back low she would need to alert the resident on call right away.

"Oh, and the patient asked me to keep her curtains drawn," added Mimi. "She seems very shy to me. This is probably her first time admitted to a hospital. I know you have to make a visual check every hour on the night shift, but maybe she won't mind the curtains being drawn back, there won't be any visitors to see her, anyway."

"I'll take care of it," Catherine said in a curt tone, not looking up from her report.

"I just don't want your rounds compromised by not having a line of sight on the patient. It could be—"

"I said I'll take care of it." Catherine circled a note on her report sheet, again not looking up at her friend. Mimi was surprised, she had never seen the night nurse speak to her so abruptly. Mimi wondered if there were problems at home. Perhaps baby Lilly still wasn't sleeping through the night, which meant mom wasn't sleeping, either. Or it could be a quarrel with the husband over their finances, Mimi knew money was tight, with Catherine's husband Louis having trouble finding steady full-time work. She decided not to press her friend, if Cathy wanted to share her troubles, she would. If not, let it ride.

"Well, you have a good night. I hope you'll be able to report to me in the morning on every patient, 'Quiet night, slept well, no complaints.'"

As Mimi went to the staff lounge to retrieve her purse and coat, she saw Catherine remaining seated at the nursing station, as if she didn't want to start her shift. As if the twelve-hour night tour was too long and too depressing to even begin.

<>

Settling into bed, Lenny tugged at the top sheet and blanket to free them from the bottom of the bed. He stuck his fee out to "let them breathe," a practice Patience had wondered about for years, since her husband's feet were not particularly malodorous. He was actually rather meticulous about his personal hygiene, using a strong soap with an exfoliant every day in the shower and always keeping his nails short.

"Dear?" he said, fluffing his pillow and getting comfortable.

"Yes?"

"About the football thing."

"What about it?" Patience's voice took on a sharp tone, a sign the conversation was not going to go in his favor.

"I understand about the danger of concussions and head injuries and all. But they don't even tackle at his age, it's more tag, you're it. I don't see the harm in it."

"Lenny." Patience reached out, grabbed his chin and turned him to face her. He hated when she did that. "A lot of the brain damage comes from when their head hits the ground in a tackle, it's not just from a direct hit to the head. Even with a helmet, they still suffer brain trauma. I've seen the x-rays and I've heard the radiologists going over the findings. Malcolm could show symptoms years and years later. It is scary shit, Lenny."

"I realize that. It's just—"

"Wait a minute! If Malcolm plays on the junior football team, he's going to want to play on the team the next year. And the next year, and the next. Then he'll want to play in high school, and then *college*. You can't tell me they don't tackle you and slam you down hard on the ground in *those* games."

"Yeah, I guess."

"That means we have to nip it in the bud. Let him play soccer. Or baseball. Baseball would be fine."

Lenny grumbled but conceded her point. He promised to explain it all to Malcolm one more time in the morning over breakfast.

"That class action grievance I filed today?" he said. "The administration is going to shit bricks when they get the paperwork."

"They've got a lot of nerve, denying parents in the LGBT community their paid leave. Can they get away with it?"

He explained how the union contract was badly outdated, the parental leave policy had been negotiated long before gay marriage was legal. The hospital policy required that the parent be the biological mother or father, and neither of them could claim that title. "I think they're going to turn us down at the third step, and in the end we'll have it to an arbitration court."

"Won't that take a long time?"

"A year, maybe two, it depends on how much they're willing to fight the ruling when they lose. Hell, they can take it all the way to the Supreme Court, even though an arbitration ruling is supposed to be final. The way those Neanderthals on the Supreme Court feel about gays and lesbians, we might win in arbitration and lose the case in the courts."

She asked if the union was going to organize protests and ask for community support. He assured her they were going to mobilize as many supporters as they could, knowing that disputes were won in the street, not in the conference room. It was all a matter of mobilizing members and their supporters and sending a message loud and clear.

Patience turned out her bedside light. "Those bastards never run out of ways to screw a hospital worker, do they?"

"Nope." He kissed her gently on the cheek, then took up the Daily News and caught up on the news, starting with the sports section. By the time he'd read all there was to read about the Eagles and the young football season, he was sleepy. The issues facing him receded to a compartment in his mind that was never completely shut, but dim enough for him to close his eyes and go to sleep.

He turned on his side, put an arm around his sleeping wife, and thanked his lucky stars she was still keeping him in her and the children's life. Still married, still welcome in her bed.

7

After giving the nurse's aide, Louisa, her assignment for the night, including allowing Clair Bowen to have her curtains drawn around the bed, Catherine loaded up her rolling medication cart with supplies and began her first rounds. Her patients were at the far end of the ward, the other RN being assigned to the first section closest to the nursing station.

She looked in on Mister Mulcahy, an older man with leg pains and chronic ulcers from diabetes and compromised circulation to the extremities. The nurses and doctors had been begging him to give up smoking, explaining that he could keep his cigarettes or his legs, but he couldn't keep them both. Finally, the patient agreed to go on a regimen of a strong anti-anxiety agent and a sedative to keep him calm while he struggled to quit smoking. The drugs were helping, but he still craved his nicotine.

"Can't sleep, Mister Mulcahy?"

"I've been chewing on toothpicks and sucking candies, but I still want a damn smoke!"

"I know, smoking is the hardest drug habit to kick. Harder than heroin, even. I'll give you an extra sleeping pill." She pulled the medication from her cart, dropped it in a paper cup and handed it to the patient with a cup of water.

"Pity I can't take it down with a little whiskey."

Catherine tossed the empty medication cup in the trash. "I'm afraid the hospital stopped stocking *spiritus fermenti* long before I became a nurse, those days are long gone. Sorry."

She left his room and checked her watch. Three minutes to ten. If she hurried, she'd be able to complete her hourly rounds before ten-twenty, the arbitrary limit imposed by

Mother Burgess, the Director of Nursing. With the GPS unit around her neck tracking her every movement, Catherine knew there would be a computer record of her rounds, and a trip to the Director's office if she missed the deadline.

Reaching Clair's room, 735, she quietly parted the curtains drawn across the bed and looked in. The patient was sitting up in bed reading something on her cell phone.

"How's the stomach tonight?" asked Catherine.

"It's okay, thank you."

"Would you like a cup of tea with milk and honey?"

"Oh, okay, that would be nice, thank you."

Catherine had a carafe of hot water on the top of her cart. She poured out a cup, dropped in a tea bag, pulled out a packet of honey and a creamer from her lab coat pocket, and set them on the bedside table. "I have to tell you, the phlebotomy tech will be by at midnight to draw your blood. We have to monitor your Hematocrit and Hemoglobin to determine if you are still bleeding."

"That's all right, I expect to be stuck a bunch more times before you let me go home."

As Clair turned her attention back to her cell phone, Catherine closed the curtains and continued on her rounds.

<>

When Catherine was starting her twelve o'clock medication rounds, she spotted Boris Nasir, the night supervisor for Housekeeping and Transportation coming out of the linen closet. The supervisor was a thickly built man with thinning gray hair that he combed across the top of his head. He had a reputation for an unpleasant body odor and an insulting way of talking to the workers under his jurisdiction.

Nasir asked the nurse if she had seen Margie, the float housekeeper. Catherine didn't want to get a worker in trouble, but at the same time, she was uncomfortable telling an outright lie.

"I think so. I think I saw someone when I was in the med room loading up my cart."

"The linens haven't been delivered." He looked at his watch. "On the night shift the housekeeper is supposed to have the closet restocked by eleven o'clock. I want you to page me if she does not restock the closet within the next hour. Is that clear?"

"All right," said Catherine, though she had no intention of reporting anybody. Nasir wasn't her direct supervisor, though he could make life difficult for her by talking dirt to the nursing supervisor on nights — something he was all too well known to do. The nurse decided to continue giving vague answers and stay out of Nasir's way.

The man walked down the hall toward Seven-North, no doubt going to check the linen closet on the sister ward.

Catherine wondered why there were people who needed to make trouble for others, and why they always seemed to end up in a management position.

Continuing her midnight rounds looking in on every one the patients under her care and dispensing medications, Catherine was relieved to see the float Housekeeper Margie at the linen closet restocking the shelves. Margie was talking with Louisa, who had was loading her own cart with linen and soap, getting ready to clean an incontinent patient. As the nurse's aide topped up her cart, Margie asked Catherine how the baby was doing. Catherine told her baby Lilly was beginning to take solid food and doing just fine.

"Got any new pictures?" asked Margie.

The nurse took out her cell phone and showed Margie and Louisa the latest photos, including a short video of Louis throwing a spongy ball to Lilly. Lilly grabbed for the ball, she didn't actually catch it, but she threw it back and chortled with glee as the dad extolled her athletic abilities.

"He's such a good daddy," said Louisa.

"Louis bought her an Eagles T-shirt to wear. He thinks by the time she's old enough for sports, girls will be playing tackle football."

"That is c-razy," said Margie. "*Nobody* should play that sport, boys or girls, it's as violent as boxing!"

When Catherine warned Margie that Mr. Nasir was looking for her and threatening to make trouble, Margie cursed loud enough that the nurse pointed at the GPS unit hanging from her neck.

"I don't give a rat's ass who hears me," Margie said. "That man is natural born evil. You know he denied me my maternity leave on account of I'm not the biological mother? Swear to god, if he don't grant me my leave, I'm gonna put a hurt on him big time!"

"Amen to that," Louisa added. But the mention of the supervisor's name still spurred both women to get on with their work, leaving Catherine to park her medication cart and write her first nursing notes of the night.

8

Seated at the nursing station, Catherine stretched out her arms and yawned. It was 2 AM, half way through her twelve-hour shift. The other RN on duty had gone back to the lounge for a cat nap, and Catherine wished she could close her eyes, too. But with her luck, Nasir would come lurking around and spot her.

She took up her flashlight and began hourly rounds, looking in each room and shining the light on each patient's chest to be sure there was breath. And life. Catherine was half-way through her hourly rounds when she reached Clair's room, 735. Parting the curtains, she shone her flashlight over the bed and saw the blanket pulled up high over a humpy form in the bed. Since the nurse needed to be sure the patient was breathing normally, she focused her light on the chest area. But after a long minute she saw no rise and fall of a chest beneath the blanket. Stepping closer, she moved the light up to the head, then gasped in surprise.

Instead of a head, there was only a balled-up bedspread.

Catherine carefully pulled back the top sheet and blanket, revealing a series of pillows arranged to resemble a body in the bed. The intravenous pump had been turned off, the intravenous catheter hanging loose at the side of the bed.

"Oh, dear," Catherine said. "This is going to be trouble."

She hurried to the bathroom to see if the patient was on the toilet.

Nobody there.

She opened the patient closet and found the plastic bag supplied in the Emergency Room with Clair's soiled clothes still in it. On top of the bag she found a patient gown, presumably the gown the patient had been wearing before she eloped.

"Houston, we have a problem," she whispered, more to herself than to the dispatcher.

"What was that you said?" the dispatcher asked through the GPS unit.

"Uh, dispatch, you better page the night administrator. And call security, too, one of our patients seems to have eloped."

"Ten-four," said the dispatcher. Catherine had never heard the phrase 'ten-four' used in the hospital before. The man must be ex-military.

She felt a sense of doom creeping over her, having no doubt that Mother Burgess, the heartless Director of Nursing, was sure to blame the night nurse for the patient's elopement, as well as any misadventure that might have visited the shy young woman. A woman with an active GI bleed wandering down Germantown Ave was in grave danger of going into shock...and dying.

Leaving Clair's empty room, Catherine found Louisa and asked if she'd seen the patient in the hallway. The aide had not seen her or anybody else walking in the hall. The other RN and the second aide came out of the nursing lounge and joined the search.

Together, the four of them went room to room searching for the missing woman. By the time the administrator on duty, Boris Nasir and a security guard arrived, the nursing staff had inspected all the rooms, including the staff lounge, and even the storage closet.

No Clair Bowen.

Catherine showed Supervisor Nasir and the security guard the empty room and the pillows arranged to look like a patient in the bed. Nasir was dumbfounded.

The night supervisor repeated the same search that Catherine and the other nursing staff had conducted. The security guard assisting him paged Joe West, Director of

James Madison Security. The young guard was anxious about having to make the call, since West had a reputation for chewing guards out and terminating the ones who didn't follow his orders immediately and fully. But the young guard knew that not paging the boss right away would be suicide.

West answered his page inside of one minute, which led the young guard to wonder if the man slept with his cell phone beside him in bed. Informed of the pillows arranged to mimic a patient in the bed, West demanded to speak with Nasir, who was the Administrator on duty. He asked Nasir if they had searched the entire ward *and* Seven North. Informed that they would be sure to search the sister unit, West told him to block off the patient's room and not let anybody enter until he could examine it. Nasir was to gather all of the guards on duty and begin a complete search of the entire facility, starting on the eighth floor and working their way down to the basement. West then asked Nasir if he had notified the police yet.

"Police?" said Nasir. "What do I have to call the police about?"

"Because when a patient elopes, they may be in danger of their life. A confused patient could be wandering the streets in the dark. An addict may be out looking for a fix."

Nasir asked Catherine if Clair was confused or a drug addict. The nurse assured him the young woman was neither and that her vital signs had been perfectly stable. Despite the information, Joe West ordered Nasir to notify the police immediately and to pull all the video feeds for the ward and for the entrances and exits to the building. "I'll be there in twenty-five minutes," West added and hung up before Nasir could reply.

Nasir stood a moment at the nursing station with the dead phone in his hand. For the arrogant housekeeping supervisor, it was one of those rare moments when he'd come up against a boss was an even bigger prick than he was.

Nasir ordered the security guard, now joined by four more officers, to search the entire facility top to bottom. Then he followed Catherine back to the nursing station. The look on his face carried disdain and anger. "How in god's name can you lose a patient? How could you let her slip through your fingers! I mean, the hallway is a straight line, you can see everything from the fucking nursing station!"

"But Mister Nasir, I have to go into the rooms to care for my patient. Some of them require ten, fifteen minutes of care. I can't see the hallway from inside a room!"

"That's no excuse, you are responsible for your patient's safety. If she became confused and disoriented, if she wandered off, anything could happen to her. She could be hit by traffic on Germantown Ave, or attacked by a mugger or a rapist."

Catherine tried to point out that the patient could hardly have been confused if she had taken the time to stuff pillows under the blanket and try to fool the nurse into thinking she was still in bed.

"If it *was* the patient who put the pillows into the bed," Nasir said.

"What? What do you mean?" said Catherine.

"I'm not convinced it was the patient who arranged the pillows in the bed." He threw Catherine a withering look.

"Of course she did. Who else would do it?"

"A guilty nurse might try to make it look like the patient was playing games. She might try to shift the blame off herself."

Catherine was so shocked at the accusation she couldn't speak. Taking her silence as a sign of guilt, Nasir leaned in on the nurse close enough she could smell the cigarette odor on his breath. "On the other hand, if somebody abducted your patient under the threat of violence, I suppose that person or persons could have stuffed the pillows in the bed and taken her away."

Catherine shuddered at the thought of any harm coming to her patient. Not a sweet, gentle frightened woman like Clair. For the moment the fear for her patient overshadowed the fear she felt for her own nursing career.

9

After paging the computer technician on-call, Joe West, chief of hospital security, demanded the man "get his ass over to the hospital right away and cue up the surveillance video recordings from Seven South, the ER and the main entrance for the night." Twenty minutes later, West arrived at the IT department in the basement, ran his ID card over the monitor mounted on the wall beside the door and listened for the click indicating the door was unlocked. He stepped into the room, where he found a sleepy technician at a computer terminal, a giant cup of coffee on the desk. The Security Chief approached the technician, a young man from Uzbekistan with a pony tail and a droopy mustache named Ali Patel.

"You have the videos cued up?" West asked.

"Yes sir, I have them all ready. What's going on, if you don't mind my asking."

"I do mind. Your job is to carry out orders, not ask questions."

"It's just that I might be able to do my job more efficiently if I knew what you were looking for."

"A patient eloped some time before two AM last night. From room seven thirty-five. Young, white female, blonde hair. I need to know what time she left the ward and where she went."

The tech called up the video recording for Seven-South, saying, "As I'm sure you know, we have one security camera trained at the nursing station. We don't have a second camera at the far end of the hall. That is where room seven thirty-five would be."

As the video feed played in real time just after the 7:30 PM report, West watched Catherine loading her medication cart and then moving it slowly down the hall and out of sight of the camera. As other staff members took up supplies and began their shift, West instructed the tech to speed up the camera. He watched Catherine come back to the medication room, then hurry back down the hall. The second RN followed a similar pattern, though the first rooms she visited were close enough to the nursing station to show her entering and leaving a few patient rooms.

"Keep going," West said. The video continued, showing the aides coming past, the nurses returning their med carts, working at the station, chatting between themselves. One nurse stepped out of view and returned moments later with two cups, he assumed of coffee or tea. West continued watching until the moment when Catherine hurried to the nursing station, picked up the phone and reported the missing patient. A short time later Nasir and a security guard came on the scene.

There was no sign of Clair Bowen leaving the unit, or of any unexplained visitor passing the station.

West ordered the technician to run the video for the main hospital entrance. He watched as staff came up the steps to begin their shift, then, later, saw staff leaving. Clair Bowen did not leave the hospital by the main entrance. Another viewing of the Emergency Room entrance showed ambulances coming with their patients, employees coming in to start their shift or leaving, a worker making the occasional run to one of the fast food joints down the street and returning, but again, no sign of Clair Bowen.

Stifling a yawn, Ali asked if the chief of security wanted to review any other video feeds. West stood a moment staring at the blank computer screen. Finally he said, "Bring up Seven North, same time period." He remained standing as the video came up on the screen and another set of workers began their shift.

<>

After reviewing the video recordings of Seven North, Seven South and the entrances to the hospital, Joe West spoke to the police captain in charge of the local precinct, a man he had worked with when he was on the force before taking the security position at James Madison. There was no sign of the missing patient so far, but the police officer promised to press the officers on patrol to keep a sharp lookout for a sick woman, possibly in a hospital gown and robe, wandering the streets. They also promised to visit her home, West having called up the information from the hospital database, in the off chance she had made it back.

West had just returned to his office when the secretary handed him a note: one of the dispatchers on the graveyard shift had overheard a comment he thought could be serious. The security chief read the note, saw that a housekeeper on last night's tour had "sworn to put a big time hurt on Ralph Nasir," one of the more unpopular supervisors. West made a mental note to speak to the dispatcher another time, it was always prudent to collect dirt on a worker, he never knew when it would come in handy. Especially when he was sparring with that pesky union steward, Lenny Moss.

10

Mimi had seen her friend Catherine look frightened in the past, but as they sat together at the nursing station for morning report, the night nurse looked even more fearful than when she'd been pregnant and exposed to the virulent strain of the Zika virus, potentially putting her newborn baby at risk or terrible deformities.

"Cath, what's the matter, you look white as a sheet!"

"Oh, Mimi, I'm in such deep doo-doo. My patient Clair Bowen, the GI bleeder, remember?"

"Sure, I admitted her, what happened? She didn't die, did she, the patient was totally stable when I handed her over."

"No, she didn't die. I mean, I don't think so." Seeing Mimi had no idea what was going on, Catherine continued. "I was making my two AM rounds, right on time, like always. I was waiting for the results of her latest H&H, she had a midnight blood draw, and when I went into her room and parted the curtains, she was gone! Poof, disappeared!"

"Say what? That's k-razy! Did she leave the hospital?"

"I don't know, nobody will tell me anything, except that I'm responsible and Mother Burgess is going to fire me and have my license revoked. Oh, god in heaven, Mimi, what will I do if I lose this job? I don't even have a union to stand up for me, and Louis is only getting part-time work."

"Okay, now, don't give in to despair. You have friends at James Madison. Good friends. Other nurses who will stand up for you. Doctors who respect your work. Patients, even, who love how you treated them."

"Are they going to testify for me when I go before the licensing board?"

"Of course they will, they'll be glad to, if it comes to that, which I *definitely* believe it won't. And don't forget, you have Lenny Moss to help you out. Remember how he saved Pauline her job when she was in trouble? He'll take care of you, I know it."

"Well, I'm going to need all the help I can get, I have to report to Miss Burgess's office soon as I finish report."

"Try not to worry. Just tell her what happened and then go on home. I'll tell Lenny and we'll figure something out."

Catherine got up from the desk and went to the staff lounge to retrieve her coat and purse. When she walked toward the elevator, she looked like a condemned prisoner on her way to the gallows. And knowing it was Mother Burgess who would do the hanging, the despondent nurse realized she had no hope of a reprieve.

<>

As soon as Mimi had her medication cart set up and given the aide her assignment, she hurried to find Lenny. But she had a problem. The dispatcher was sure to hear every word she said thanks to the hated GPS unit suspended around her neck. Turning it off or removing it while on duty without a really good reason was immediate grounds for termination, as more than one RN had learned to her dismay.

So Mimi wrote a note on a blank piece of paper. She found Lenny in a patient bathroom cleaning the floor of a man with explosive diarrhea. The poor man was waiting for approval of a "stool transplant," a sample of stool loaded with benign microorganisms that would re-seed his infected gut. But his doctor was having trouble finding a safe donor, the patient had no wife and his daughter was living in California.

Holding a finger to her lips to let Lenny know he was to keep silent, Mimi took the note from her lab coat pocket and held it out to him.

Lenny put his mop in the bucket and carefully read the note: "PATIENT CLAIR BOWEN DISAPPEARED

DURING NIGHT, ROOM 735, CATHERINE AFRAID WILL BE FIRED, NEEDS HELP.

Lenny thought for a moment. Then he asked the nurse if the "discharge" bed in 735 had been cleared and cleaned. Mimi shook her head no. "Okay, I'll get right on cleaning the room for an admission." Mimi gave Lenny a thumbs up, knowing he would not be cleaning the room, he would be investigating it.

Lenny rolled the mop and bucket out to the hall and made his way to Clair Bowen's room. He stood a moment in the doorway, looking at the curtain drawn across the bed and thinking. Had Catherine or Mimi drawn the curtain? If they did, why? For just a second he imagined what it would be like to track a missing person in a wood, searching for footprints in the soft earth and signs of passage in broken branches. That was in the movies and TV, he told himself. What kind of a trail would a patient leave in a hospital?

He stepped in and parted the curtain. The top sheet and bedspread were roughly piled at the foot of the bed. A line of pillows filled the space a patient's body would have taken up. A bundle of bedspread tied in a rough circular shape sat where the head would be. It was crude, but in a dim light with the top sheet and bedspread pulled high up, it might well fool a busy nurse who was just looking in from the doorway.

Why fake an occupant in the bed? Time to escape, maybe. But who was doing the escaping, the patient or the perpetrator?

Lenny stepped to the bed and examined the bottom sheet. It was clean, with no blood stains or stool. He knew that an active GI bleeder would likely have left some spots of blood or black, tarry stool behind, having cleaned up many a soiled bed over the years.

Curiouser and curiouser.

He examined the overbed table. It had a partially eaten bowl of Jello and a half-empty cup of tea, a diet consistent with a GI bleeder. The bedside cabinet held a bible, a breakfast menu not filled out, a little pencil and an unused washrag and towel.

Unused towel. A GI bleeder would have been bathed when she came to the ward. Maybe these were a spare set.

He opened the closet. The plastic clothing bag from the ER was sealed. He opened it and looked inside, found a woman's sweater with a serious amount of blood on it, a bra (clean), pants with spots of blood, shoes and socks. He found no purse, cell phone, wallet or other personal belongings.

He noted that none of those items had been in the bedside cabinet, either.

Finished examining the room, Lenny went to the bathroom, where there were no blood stains in the sink, and none in the toilet. He considered that even if any bloody or tarry stool had been flushed away, there should still be traces of blood on the bowl, a GI bleed always brought on diarrhea, and the night housekeeping staff only cleaned discharge rooms, so the room would not have been cleaned.

He saw, too, that the shower had not been used, the bar of soap was still wrapped in its paper cover, so no bathing had occurred here.

The trash bucket in the bathroom was empty.

Lenny stood a moment in the middle of the room giving it one last look. There was no indication of a violent struggle. The pillows masquerading as a body suggested the patient had tried to conceal her departure as long as possible, unless a perpetrator had set up the humpy bed to gain time for removing the patient. Or the body.

Lenny didn't want to rule out foul play, he knew that a violent hand was always a possibility. With all of the greed and cruelty in this world, it was always prudent to look for the mark of an evil doer.

As Lenny turned to leave, he almost collided with Boris Nasir, the midnight supervisor for Housekeeping and Messenger Service. Nasir was notorious for insulting workers to their face and writing them up for the most petty transgressions, Lenny had filed many a grievance against him over the years.

"What are you doing in the room, Moss?" Nasir stood with his legs slightly bent and apart, as if he was a linebacker getting ready to hit the running back and knock him down.

"This is a discharge room, isn't it?"

"Not according to Admissions. Did the nurse tell you to clean the room?"

"Actually, she told me she didn't know when I should strip the bed and clean it, only that it would probably be some time on my shift. I wanted to see how big a job it's gonna be, these GI bleeders can leave a shit load of bloody stool to clean up. I remember the time when—"

"Cut the crap! You better not be sticking your big nose into matters that don't concern you."

"My nose resents your characterization," Lenny replied, trying to deflect Nasir with humor. When the wily custodian protested he had no idea what the man was talking about, Nasir said with a sneer, "You're wasting your time with that bull shit paternity leave grievance. Read the fucking contract, your fag friends don't have a leg to stand on. You'll drop the whole god damned thing if you know what's good for you."

"Actually, Margie is lesbian, but thanks for the advice. I've always been a sucker for lost causes, but I'll be sure to take it under advisement."

As Lenny started walking down the hall, Nasir called after him with a warning: if he caught the steward snooping around things that were outside his union responsibilities, he'll be suspended faster than a bullet can find its target.

Lenny was happy to go, having learned some useful information. if Nasir was examining the missing patient's room *and* trying to keep Lenny from looking into the affair, that meant this case was a serious incident. The bosses were definitely worried about *something*: bad publicity, a lawsuit, a fatal medical error.

Something.

He didn't like being threatened and he didn't like Nasir. Returning to his work, Lenny was determined to get to the bottom of things. And he had a good idea where he would look next.

11

When Catherine stepped into Miss Burgess's office and saw Boris Nasir standing beside the dour Director of Nursing, she realized she was in the worst trouble of her life. A single straight-backed chair was placed in front of the Director's huge cherry wood desk. She knew that would be her place of execution.

"Sit down, Missus Feekin," Burgess ordered. She was a broad-beamed, middle-aged woman. Her thick lips were often wet with spit, and she wore heavy pancake makeup that gave her an unhealthy look. The nurses joked when off duty and not wearing the hated GPS unit that Burgess was really one of the Undead and needed to be stuffed back in her grave at night.

None of the silver rings on her fingers were wedding bands. She was married to the job.

"I have here in my hand your incident report. It says that you conducted your hourly rounds as usual, and that you saw no indication that the patient would leave the facility. Do you stand by that statement?"

"Yes, ma'am, that's correct."

"Except your report is *not* correct. The computer tracking of your GPS unit clearly shows that you were extremely late finishing your midnight rounds. You did not give your last two AM medication until..." She peered down at a computer printout. "Until two fifty-eight, which is considerably past the acceptable time to administer the medication."

She looked up at Catherine expecting a tearful confession of guilt.

"But Miss Burgess, when I found Miss Bowen missing, I couldn't very well continue my rounds as if nothing had happened, could i? I mean, I had to look for her, didn't I?"

"You spent all of thirty minutes conducting a search that you should have left to the security department and the night supervisor. Your patients went without care that entire time. You abandoned them! This is a serious, serious case of unprofessional behavior."

Catherine had expected she would find no support from the Director, but this accusation was unexpected. And shocking. She waited for the inevitable conclusion, knowing how Mother Burgess treated nurses she didn't like or trust.

"You are suspended beginning today. Human resources will conduct a full review of your case, and when that is concluded you will receive a final written statement as to your employment status."

As Catherine slowly stood up to leave, Burgess added, "And I wouldn't be too quick to look for another job in the nursing field. I will be reporting your behavior to the licensure board, you can expect to hear from them in due course."

Seeing that Burgess had no further interest in talking or listening to Catherine, the weary night nurse slowly rose from her chair and walked to the door, determined not to cry in front of the hated supervisor. She would save her tears for her husband and her darling baby girl.

<>

At morning break time, Lenny stopped at the nursing station, where Mimi was writing her first notes of the day. He pantomimed sewing a needle and thread, letting her know he would be in the sewing room. Mimi held up her hand with five fingers extended, so he knew she would be down in five minutes.

Grabbing a coffee and a donut in the cafeteria, Lenny hurried to the sewing room, the unofficial meeting place for union troublemakers. He found Birdie seated at her usual station running a sheet through the big industrial sewing machine. Her husband was sitting backwards in a battered old folding chair, his chin resting on the back of the chair.

Lenny took a bite out of the donut, glanced over at Moose and raised a single dark eyebrow, daring his friend to make a comment. Moose just shook his head, not bothering to ask why Lenny *never* dunked his donut, he knew the man was a hopeless case. A donut purist.

"You take the stairs comin' down here this morning?" asked Moose, who for years had been haranguing his friend to get more exercise. He even dragged Lenny out to Fairmont Park on the weekend to go jogging, usually having to listen to a series of protests before Lenny agreed to meet him there.

"Yes, I took the stairs. And it's not easy opening the door with coffee in one hand and a donut in the other."

"Hold it in your mouth, be no problem," Moose deadpanned, bringing a grin to his wife's face.

"What's up with you, Lenny?" Birdie asked. He told her he had filed a grievance for Margie and Woody over denial of paid paternity leave. Birdie asked how could they get away with that, discriminating on account of someone's sex or sexual orientation was against the law as far as she understood it.

"We have an outdated contract," he said. "It was written before same-sex marriage was legalized, so our contract doesn't require paid leave for gay or lesbian parents, at least, when they aren't the biological parent."

"We're gonna change that the next contract, aren't we?" said Moose.

"We'll certainly put it on the table. But you know how those bastards are, they fight us over everything. If we lose the grievance I'm hoping we can beat them in court, I'm supposed to meet one of the union lawyers this afternoon."

A knock on the door turned their heads. Mimi poked her head in. "Are you sure the dispatcher can't hear me down here, Lenny? You remember what happened the last time I opened my mouth down the sewing room."

Lenny assured the nurse this time she was safe in their basement hideaway. A year ago, the union had found a hidden relay unit concealed in the sewing room ceiling, a sneaky tactic that allowed the dispatcher to listen in to the nurse's GPS unit as long as he kept his own microphone on mute. When the union threatened a million dollar lawsuit for invasion of privacy, the unit was removed. Lenny was confident that this time Mimi's GPS unit would not transmit or receive in the basement sewing room.

Pulling open an old metal folding chairs, Mimi told Lenny that Mother Burgess had suspended Catherine and was going for final termination. She was bound to try getting her license revoked as well.

"And she's got no union to defend her," Moose added.

Mimi reminded Moose that she had tried to get the nurses to sign up with their service workers union, but too many wanted to go with the UNP, the union of Pennsylvania "professional nurses." She turned to Lenny and asked what had he learned so far about Clair Bowen, the patient that had disappeared. He told her there were no signs that the patient had used the bathroom to wash up or had used the toilet. That went against his experience cleaning the bathrooms of GI bleeders.

Mimi agreed. She told them that Dr. Stone suspected the patient had a nosebleed, not a bleeding gastric ulcer. "That would explain why her hemoglobin and hematocrit were pretty much to normal," she added. "Nosebleeds don't usually drop your 'crit the way a full-blown bleeding stomach ulcer does."

She asked if he thought the patient had left on her own, or if somebody took her. Lenny said there wasn't enough evidence to come to any conclusion, but the pillows arranged under the blanket that made it look like a body was still there suggested the patient had planned to slip out. Whether Clair planned it on her own or somebody else brought the pillows in as part of an abduction, he couldn't say.

"The curtains were closed around the bed when I went to look at it," said Lenny. "Were they pulled shut after the patient eloped?"

Mimi told him how Clair had asked that her curtains be kept drawn across the bed, supposedly for privacy. The nurse assumed the patient was shy, but now she suspected the patient had other reasons for staying out of sight. "She could have been hiding from somebody."

"Or she was hiding from the staff while she made up the phony bed," Birdie suggested. "That's what I'd have done if I was gonna skip out before anybody saw me."

Lenny complained that without more information, he couldn't do much to defend the night nurse from her impending termination.

"So is that it?" asked Mimi. "That's the end of it? That's all you're gonna *do* for her?"

Birdie looked at Moose, who said, "You know ain't nobody's giving up. We'll all help out, like we always do. We're the eyes and ears of the hospital, there's nothin' that happens at James Madison, one of us service workers isn't around to see it. We just need to know what we're looking for."

Lenny assured Mimi he had just begun working on the case. He had several people to talk to, it was early days.

Mimi got up to leave, saying, "I'm afraid it's late at night, Lenny, and the sun is setting on Catharine."

<>

Before returning to Seven South, Lenny made a stop at the IT department, which was a stone's throw down the hall from the sewing room. He went back and found his friend, Ali at his station with a large cup of coffee and an egg & cheese sandwich half eaten on the computer desk. Another even larger empty coffee cup was in the trash bucket beside the desk.

On the desk beside the computer monitor was a framed picture of a newborn baby girl, small and frail and helpless. Seeing the familiar picture, Lenny felt a pang of sadness, recalling the time when Ali's daughter had been born prematurely and with life-threatening congenital abnormalities. The baby had survived for twenty-two days in the NICU. The marriage hadn't lasted much longer than that.

"Out drinking again last night?" Lenny asked, having noted the two coffee cups.

"Hey, Lenny. No, Joe West called me in at three-thirty in the morning. It felt like I was back on the graveyard shift."

Lenny said he was sorry for the early hours, then he explained he was trying to help the nurse facing termination over the disappearing patient. Since he couldn't spend a lot of time in the IT department, would Ali make copies of the video feed for both wards, the ER, main entrance and the loading dock. With a long yawn, the tech told him it was no problem, give him some time, he'd get the files to Lenny later in the day.

About to leave, Lenny noted a rather large bottle of ibuprofen on Ali's desk. "What's with the pain killers? You had an injury? Need to file workman's comp or something?"

"No, thanks, man, it's these damn headaches. They've been getting worse and worse. I can't hardly sleep at night."

Lenny sat down again and studied his friend's face, saw pain etched in his eyes and brow. "It sounds serious, you see a doctor?"

"No, but I will, I've just been crazy busy. I'll make an appointment this week."

"You damn well better. I'm gonna check back with you in a couple of days, make sure you saw somebody. And thanks for helping with the video."

Worried about Ali's health, Lenny hurried back to Seven South, taking the elevator this time and not the stairs, as Moose was always haranguing him to do to stay in shape. He had no time, and he was already weary as hell.

12

At 2:45 PM, Lenny was putting away his mop and bucket when Carlton came up to the housekeeping locker pushing his delivery cart. "Yo, Lenny, how's it hanging?" the young messenger said. He was a tall, gangly fellow with an eternal smile on his lips that Lenny knew had nothing to do with drugs or alcohol.

"It's crap any way you look at it," Lenny said. "How's by you?"

"My life could not be better. Doctor Auginello has somebody looking at my idea about changing your breath to keep the mosquitoes from tracking you. It could be a monster medical breakthrough!"

"That's great, Carlton. I'm happy one of your brainstorms might work out this time."

"Yeah, thanks, I'm psyched. But I still got a lotta other great ideas. I've been thinking about the climate crisis, see, and how the droughts are getting so bad and all. And I came up with a way to float an iceberg from Antarctica to, like, South Africa or Australia."

"Yeah, I've seen the articles in The Guardian, but it would take a gazillion gallons of diesel fuel to power a ship big enough to tow it, and that's not good for planet earth, either."

Carlton grinned a big, infectious grin. "I got a better way. I'm gonna use big-ass sails to harness the wind, it blows north like all get out from the South Pole. Gonna let the wind push the berg all the way to Australia!"

Lenny didn't want to discourage his friend, who had come up with a lot of goofy "inventions" in the past, so he just smiled and wished him good luck. When Carlton put out his hand to shake, Lenny, puzzled, extended his open hand. Inside the handshake, Carlton, slipped him a thumbnail drive. Lenny understood right away that Carlton had picked it up on his Messenger rounds from Ali, and that the drive contained digital files of the video recording on the wards the night Clair Bowen disappeared.

"Enjoy the movie," Carlton said and headed off, pushing his cart and dreaming of saving the planet.

Lenny dropped the drive in his shirt pocket and watched his friend leave, grateful, as he had felt so many times before, at having so many good friends and brothers in the struggle like Ali and Carlton. He just wished he had more of Carlton's perennial optimism. But Lenny had seen too much cruelty in the world, whether from the bosses who administered their arrogant idea of justice, or the workers who took out their suffering on each other.

<>

After rinsing the bucket and hanging up the mop head to dry, Lenny left the ward and met his wife at the main entrance to the hospital. On the drive home he filled her in on the events of the day.

"Good lord," said Patience. "That's the worst news I've heard in years: a patient elopes, maybe she was abducted, and they suspend the *nurse*? What kind of sick people are running this hospital, anyway?"

"Just your average greedy scumbags," said Lenny.

In the house, Patience asked what was he going to do next. He told her he had to review the surveillance videos from the night shift. Then, if she didn't mind doing the homework with the kids, he wanted to drive over to Manayunk and talk to Catherine. Since she was suspended and facing termination, he promised Mimi he would do what he could to help her.

"And that means you're going to find out what happened to the missing patient?"

"If I can."

She kissed her husband on the cheek. "Of course you'll figure it out. You're the most stubborn man I know. Most of the time you're a pain in my backside, but every once in a while..."

"Once in a while what?"

"You're supposed to be the detective: you figure it out."

With Patience looking over his shoulder, Lenny opened his laptop and played the first video. They saw Catherine load up her medication cart, speak to the nurse's aide assisting her, and then pushing her cart down the hall and out of the camera's view.

With the video playing double speed, they saw the nurses and aides come in and out of the frame, but they did not see Clair Bowen pass the nursing station. Nor did they see anyone who did not clearly belong on the ward pass by. There was the nursing staff — two registered nurses and two nurse aides — a phlebotomy tech coming through to draw labs around midnight, Margie, one of the night shift housekeepers delivering linen, and a young physician, possibly a medical student, who looked through a chart at the nursing station and then went back the way he had come.

Lenny switched to the Seven North video to settle the question of where the patient had made her exit. Since the sister station was close to the connecting passage between the two wards, anyone leaving Seven South by that route would have to pass the other nursing station and be seen on video.

Again, they saw two nurses and two aides, the tech going by with her little tray for drawing blood, and Margie again delivering linen. Someone in surgical scrubs and an isolation gown, a surgical cap and a mask dangling around his neck walked by going toward Seven South. His head had been turned away from the camera and the mask covered his chin, so the face was not visible. The individual pushed a small cart that was covered with a sheet. There was no way to determine what was on the cart, or even what department the man belonged to.

They did *not* see Clair Bowen pass by the Seven North nursing station.

"Who the hell is that?" Patience asked, pointing at the figure in scrubs and surgical hat and mask.

"Beats me," Lenny said. He reversed the tape, went back and played it again.

"He's got a limp, did you see that?" Patience said.

Lenny agreed, the figure in scrubs had a slight limp. "I think there's someone on the night shift who walks with a limp." He closed his eyes and put a hand to his forehead, imagining each one of the night shift housekeeping staff. Suddenly he opened his eyes.

"It's the supervisor! Boris Nasir walks with a limp!"

Patience pointed out it didn't make sense that Nasir would be wearing a scrub suit and pushing a cart, he always wore a suit, and he spent his time pushing people around, not carts.

Curiouser and curiouser.

Lenny noted that the two videos did show that Clair had not left by way of the sister unit or from Seven South, she would have had to pass one of the nursing stations. The only other way to leave was to go by the same stairs that he walked down to get to the sewing room in the basement.

"She must have left by the exit at the end of the ward," Patience said. "It's the only other way off the ward."

"Correct."

"That makes sense. If she wanted to leave without being seen, the stairwell is the best place to do it. I bet that guy with the covered cart was bringing the pillows."

"And a change of clothes," Lenny added, telling his wife that Clair had left her bloody clothes behind in the room. "We still don't know if he was friend or foe, he might have threatened her and forced her to leave with him."

60

"Yes, but don't forget she asked to have the curtains drawn around her bed. Doesn't that prove she was setting herself up to elope?"

"Maybe not. It could mean she was simply scared. Like of somebody coming for her life."

Lenny opened the video file for the main entrance to the hospital to see if Clair and the unidentified man had exited there. He was not surprised to find no sign of either person. The other video files for the ER showed the same empty results: there was no sign of Clair or of anyone looking remotely like her leaving the hospital by any of the monitored exits.

The loading dock was closed at night, but Ali, bless his cold heart, had included the video feed for that area, and it, too, showed no sign of Clair or they mystery man in the isolation gown and surgical cap.

It was puzzling, but Lenny was not discouraged. He had dealt with all the ways that workers found to get past the system. All the ways of smuggling unapproved items into the hospital, and all the ways of sneaking hospital items out without being detected. Like the worker some years back who had smuggled chicken cutlets from the kitchen. The head chef had thrown the chicken in the garbage, the meat was past its safe to use date, but the worker took them home intending to donate them to a local soup kitchen, where they would boil the hell out of them, especially the bones. Taking the hospital food had been a big issue with the kitchen supervisor, a preening sycophant who was dying to move up the poisonous managerial food chain. The supervisor wanted to terminate the worker for stealing, so he called the police and told them the worker was in possession of stolen hospital property in his car.

Warned of the threat from the police by a co-worker in the kitchen, the worker had been a lot smarter than the boss. When the police searched his car in front of his home, they found new chicken cutlets from a local grocer, the worker had switched them before reaching his house, dropping the purloined cutlets at the church soup kitchen.

Seeing a satisfied smile on her husband's face, Patience suggested he knew just how Clair, and her male companion, had gotten away undetected. He chuckled as he told her, because the solution was a simple one, if you only understood how the workers outwitted the bosses in the James Madison health factory.

13

With dinner over and Patience leading the children upstairs to start their homework, Lenny headed for Manayunk, having visited Catherine when the RNs were trying to convince their co-workers to join Lenny's Hospital Service Workers Union. He arrived at 5 pm and hoped he wasn't be interrupting her sleep or her dinner.

The doorbell chimed. Louis came to the door, saw it was Lenny and welcomed him inside. "How you been, man?" Louis said. "Everything okay at home?"

"Yeah, fine, the kids are a pain in the ass, Malcolm wants to play junior football, but the wife is afraid he'll get a concussion."

"Yeah, she's right, that's a bad ass sport for kids. Put him on the track team. Or swimming."

"Good idea, he can hit his head on the bottom of the pool diving and drown...Listen, can I talk to Catherine? She awake?"

"Yeah, she's up. I'll tell her you're here."

Louis went to the door to the basement, walked down a step and closed the door behind him. A few minutes later he came back with Catherine behind him.

"You keeping the baby in the basement?" said Lenny. "Good idea, you won't hear her crying so much."

"Hi, Lenny," said Catherine. "Thanks so much for coming by. I guess you heard I'm suspended."

"Yes. Sorry to hear it. Have you contacted a lawyer?"

"Not yet. But I will. Tomorrow. My sister knows somebody in Center City, I have the number."

"Good, that's good. From what I've heard, you'll have a strong case. If I can help in any way..."

"I know, Lenny, thank you, I'll give the lawyer your number."

When Louis offered coffee or tea, Lenny asked if they had anything stronger.

"Jack Daniels?" Louis offered.

"Yes, thank you! Neat it fine."

As Louis poured drinks for himself and Lenny, Catherine recounted the hours when Clair Bowen had disappeared. She told him about allowing the patient to keep the curtains closed, which was unusual, she liked to have a line of sight on her patients. But some people wanted their privacy, and as long as their condition was stable and they weren't at risk of falling out of bed, they usually allowed it.

Lenny noted that the woman had not used the bathroom to clean up or to move her bowels. "GI bleeders usually need the toilet a lot. What do you make of that?"

Catherine told him that the ER physician thought it wasn't a true GI bleed, more likely a nose bleed that she'd swallowed. That was consistent with her normal Hemoglobin. And they'd done a good job cleaning her up in the ER, so perhaps she didn't need to wash up again so soon.

Lenny agreed, it all made sense. It was the disappearance that was senseless, at least so far. "Did she seem to you like she was so frightened she would run off in the middle of the night?"

"I don't know, Lenny, I just thought she was shy. Anxious, yes, but not *that* scared."

He asked Catherine if she had seen a man in a surgical gown, cap and gown come through pushing a cart. A cart that was covered. She said no, she hadn't, and asked, who was he? He told her maybe it had nothing to do with Clair's disappearing, it was just something he was checking out.

Lenny sipped his drink. He looked over at Louis, who had finished his drink already. Louis said he was going to check on the baby and went upstairs.

"Can you get work if the termination goes through?" Lenny asked.

Catherine told him she had a good friend who worked at one of the temp agencies, they would take her on, as long as she still had a license. If it came to that and she did lose her nursing license, she would work as an aide in a nursing home if she had to, somehow she and her family would pull through.

Catherine's face reddened in a blush of anger. She reported Boris Nasir's accusation that she, the *nurse*, had stuffed the pillows in the bed to justify not finding the patient missing until two in the morning."

"Nasir is a mean son of a bitch," Lenny said. "He would come up with creap like that."

"Do you think Nasir had anything to do with my patient's leaving the way she did?"

Lenny admitted he had no idea. There was no reason that he could see for the night supervisor interfering with a sick patient, but they had so little information, nothing could be ruled in or out.

Finishing his drink, Lenny got up to leave. He thanked Catherine for talking to him, and as he reached the front door, she asked him who else was he going to talk to about the incident. Lenny stopped for a moment to think.

"I'll have to talk to the float housekeeper who was covering the seventh floor. And the lab tech who was drawing blood. And of course, the nursing staff who worked with you that night. That's about it. Why?"

"No reason. I was just wondering, I know how you can dig deep into something until you get to the bottom, like you did with the case of Dr. Austin."

Averse to praise, Lenny shook Louis's hand and stepped out into the night. The air was crisp and cold, with a sharp wind from the north. Falling leaves crunches beneath his feet as he walked to his car. He couldn't avoid the gloomy thought that Clair Bowen was dead and buried in the cold, damp earth...and that Regis would have to set her up one day for the autopsy.

14

On Friday morning Lenny got to work early, he wanted to talk to Louisa, the nurse's aide who had worked on Seven South the night Clair disappeared. After pulling his time card from the rack on the wall and punching in, he looked to see if the aide was on duty. He found her card and had just lifted it far enough out of its slot to see if she had punched in the night before when a powerful hand grabbed him by the shoulder.

"You punch anther employee's time card for him it's immediate dismissal with no chance for appeal." Ralph Nasir had seen Lenny come into the department and was curious why the man was punching in a half hour before the start of his shift. The suspicious supervisor knew it could only be some pesky union activity.

Lenny pulled the arrogant man's arm away, resisting the impulse to use his other hand in a fist. "I wasn't punching anybody in or out, I was just seeing if a worker I represent was on duty this morning. It's protected union activity and you know it."

"*Protected?* There's nothing gonna protect you when I come for you, Moss. You better watch your back, 'cause you won't see it coming when the hammer comes down on that thick skull of yours."

As Nasir walked back into the office, Lenny noted, as he had several times before, that the man walked with a slight limp. He hoped whatever the disability was caused the man a lot of chronic pain.

Nasir's threat didn't bother Lenny, he was used to bullies like the arrogant night supervisor. But he also knew that management would try to take out their anger on the two workers who were named in the grievance, and Margie

with her hot temper and loud mouth was ripe for a repri-
mand. Or worse.

<>

Lenny found Louisa in the Seven South nursing lounge
swapping her white shoes for a pair of hot pink trainers.

"Nice sneaks," he said. "You gonna run in the
Philly marathon?"

"Hell, working in this dump twelve hours a night is all the
running around a body needs!" She laced up her shoes and
waited, knowing full well why Lenny was chatting her up,

"So, Louisa, Mimi asked me to look into this patient
Clair Bowen that disappeared the other night. You mind
telling me what happened?"

"Beats me, Lenny. I just clean up the patients and make
the beds. I don't know nothin' about no missing patient."

"I wasn't trying to say you did know. It's just, you have
good eyes and good ears. Did you see anybody on the ward
after midnight who maybe didn't belong? Somebody you
didn't know?"

"Nope." Louisa dropped her work shoes into a draw-
string bag and got up to put it in her locker.

"O-kay. How about the patient, Clair Bowen? How did
she seem? Did she act scared? Or depressed? Could she
have been suicidal?"

Louisa told him she didn't know much about psycholo-
gy, the only thing she could say was that the young woman had been shy, she'd asked to keep the curtains closed
around her bed, which Catherine okay'd, and she never
put her light on to ask for help.

Lenny said, "I went into the room the morning she went
missing. I didn't see any sign the patient had washed up.
The bar of soap was still in its wrapper, the towel and
washrag were clean. Why do you think she didn't wash up?
GI bleeders usually need a lot of hygiene."

Louisa shrugged her shoulders. "Guess they cleaned her up good in the ER."

Lenny waited in silence for a moment. After so many years questioning workers and supervisors, he'd learned that sometimes the most important information came if he just sat and waited. But Louis offered nothing more.

He wished Louisa a good sleep and went out to begin his duties. As he set up his mop and bucket, pouring liquid soap and bleach in the steel bucket, Lenny noted that Louisa confirmed Catherine's account of the woman being shy and wanting the curtains closed. If she had been planning to elope and needed time to set up the bed to look like she was sleeping there, keeping the curtains closed was a damn good way to do it.

But still, it could equally mean that the woman was scared of being seen. Scared of somebody.

His second observation was that Louisa had been damn cagey. She'd avoided eye contact for much of the conversation. That was unusual for her, she generally was open and friendly to him. Could be she was scared she was going to be in trouble for the patient's disappearance. But if that was the case, surely she would have shared her fears with Lenny, her union steward and, he hoped, a trusted confidante.

He thought of the old joke from the movie *Airplane!* "Don't call me Shirley!" The classics were still the best.

<>

Lenny was at the nursing station going over the scheduled discharges with Mimi when Margie hurried up to them. She asked Lenny how was the grievance going. Her face was tight with anger, Lenny could she was a firecracker waiting to go off.

He asked her to be patient, the grievance process was slow and frustrating. He told her he had a step two meeting with Mr. Freely, the Director of Human Resources scheduled for the afternoon, and he would text her about it when it was done.

He cautioned her, "Don't think the union can resolve this in just one meeting. Sometimes we can, yes, but usually we need to take it to the next step, and when it comes to paid leave, it'll probably have to go to arbitration."

"How long is that gonnna take? Man, I want to start my leave like today!"

"Your best bet is to take an unpaid leave, and when we win the case you'll get your back pay, with interest."

Margie started to curse the supervisor. She told Lenny if the hospital didn't pay her the time she was owed, she'd put a hurt on that bastard Nasir big time.

Seeing that Mimi was beside them with the GPS unit on a lanyard around her neck, Lenny asked the angry housekeeper to keep her voice down. He wished the union could make the appeal go faster, but the bosses did everything they could to drag out these issues, hoping the worker gives up. Or dies before a settlement, she'd just have to be patient. And quiet.

"The bosses got a million was to screw us, don't they, Lenny?"

"I'm afraid they do, Margie."

He watched the woman head for the elevators. She was a good worker. Never written up for being late. Never protested when she had to work a holiday. He hoped her anger didn't get out of control, the bosses were quick to fire a worker who made threatening remarks about a supervisor, and a grievance for that transgression never went well for the union. One big blow up on Margie's part would be grounds for immediate termination, and that would make it even tougher to win the grievance for parental leave.

15

When it was time for morning break Lenny took the stairs to the basement, grumbling how his friend Moose Maddox always insisted he skip the elevator and get extra exercise walking the stairs. Like he didn't get enough exercise mopping the floors and cleaning the rooms? Lenny stopped at the cafeteria for a coffee and a donut, then went down to the sewing room.

Moose was seated beside his wife, Birdie, who was working the industrial sewing machine when Lenny came in and opened a folding chair. She gave him a smile, then a scowl. "What's goin' on with the nurses, Lenny? They gonna vote for a union or what? Seems like they've been dragging their union campaign on for-ever!"

"Hell, don't ask me, ask the U-N-P. We gave up trying to organize the RNs when they handed back our pledge cards and switched to the United Nurse of Pennsylvania, the 'professional' nurses' union." Lenny added that the hospital had been relentless in their attacks on the new union drive. They made the nurses attend meetings where Mother Burgess threatened all kinds of hell and damnation if "her girls" signed with a union. And they told the nurses, falsely, as Lenny knew, that they would all lose their license to practice if they ever went on strike because they would be abandoning their patients. The truth was, striking nurses always gave management time to cut the census and hire contract nurses, but truth was something Burgess had little time for.

"They should've stuck with *our* union," said Birdie. Moose reminded his wife that the RNs supervised the aides and clerks, a lot of them didn't want their authority questioned. Lenny added that the RNs would have had their own division within the HSWU, but in the end they chose to go with the United Nurses of Pennsylvania.

Birdie shook her head as she folded a patient gown she'd repaired. "For a bunch of educated women, you'd think they wouldn't fall for that crap."

Lenny pointed out that if the nurses did succeed in their union drive — and he hoped they did — there was still a chance the two unions could work together on some issues, like workplace safety, staffing ratios and public health concerns.

Lenny bit into his donut and cast a warning glance at Moose, who chuckled but said nothing. In the past, Moose had questioned why Lenny didn't dip his donut in his coffee, saying dunking was their "destiny," but Lenny regarded dunking a sugary donut as a violation of his loyalty to the brew, which he took black, *no* sugar.

"You take the stairs this morning?" Moose asked him.

"Yes, I took the stairs," Lenny replied. "I even carried two five-gallon buckets of detergent just to increase the burn. Mopping floors and cleaning toilets and scraping shit up wasn't giving me the sculpted body that I crave."

His friend chuckled. "We're goin' jogging Saturday, don't forget."

"Yeah, yeah. You can jog, I'm gonna sit by the creek and meditate on the futility of fighting my fate. I mean—"

Knock-knock-knock.

Lenny stopped speaking as the door opened and Dr. Robert Stone stepped into the room.

"Okay if I intrude for a moment?" the ER physician asked.

"Come on in, doc, the more the merrier!" Birdie told him. Moose unfolded a metal chair and set it out for him. Stone spread his long legs out and took a breath.

"Sorry to barge in like this, but the nurse on Seven South told me I could find Lenny here, and, well, I've got something on my mind, so..."

Lenny said, "It's fine, Doctor Stone. What's it about?" Having talked with Dr. Stone on several occasions when

Lenny was called in to defend a union worker who was facing discipline, Lenny knew that the ER physician was a straight shooter and could be trusted, even with delicate issues that bent the rules a bit.

"I've been puzzling over the patient who was admitted to your ward the other night, Clair Bowen. There were some aspects of her case that didn't fit the usual diagnosis of GI bleed. I wanted to ask you about them."

"Why come to me?"

Stone told him not to indulge in false modesty. "Everybody in James Madison knows you have a nose for investigating malfeasance, Lenny."

"Hey, leave my nose out of it."

Stone reminded him that a sharp-witted steward has the ear of workers all over the hospital. Moose added that even a lot of the front line supervisors trusted him. "That's a gift, and it's a gift that you use wisely," the doctor added.

"Okay, okay," said Lenny, "What do you want to know"

"Well, for one thing, she presented in the ER vomiting blood. And she reported that her stools had been black. All consistent with a GI bleed."

"And the problem is..." said Lenny.

"The problem is, her blood count was normal. Even after tanking her up with a liter of intravenous fluids, she was still in the low-normal range. An active GI bleed always has a low hematocrit and hemoglobin. Unless she was polycythemic to begin with, but that's unlikely."

"Polycy..." Moose said.

"It's a condition where the bone marrow makes too many red cells. It's pretty rare. In theory a patient with that condition could bleed quite a lot and show a normal blood count, but it's an awfully rare disease."

"What do you think's goin' on?" asked Birdie, now no longer running the sewing machine. "Did her bleeding just stop?"

"All bleeding stops, eventually," said Stone. The implication was not lost on any of the others in the sewing room: either your bleeding ulcer healed over...or you died.

"I had her scheduled for an upper endoscopy in the morning. You know, the scope we snake down the throat. They would look for swollen varices in the esophagus and stomach, or a bleeding ulcer."

"But she disappeared before they could do the test," said Lenny.

"That's right. Given the patient disappeared from your ward, and knowing your reputation for investigating unusual events, I figured you'd be involved in this some way."

Lenny was tempted to protest that he was just a simple custodian, why did people think he had some sort of special insight into mysterious things. But after years of defending workers and even getting them out of jail by uncovering the real guilty party, Lenny had to admit it made sense for Stone to suspect he was on the case.

He told the physician he did inspect the room before it was cleaned. Clair Bowen had not used the bathroom to clean up. It looked like she hadn't used the toilet, either, there would have been dark residue in the bowl, GI bleeders were always messy. Not only that, she had arranged pillows under the blanket so it looked like she was asleep.

Stone agreed, somebody with a GI bleed would have bathed, the basin of soap and water they offered in the ER was clearly inadequate, and she would have used the toilet, probably several times.

"Where'd she get the extra pillows?" asked Birdie.

"Good point," Lenny said. He told them about the mystery man in the surgical scrub suit pushing a covered cart past the Seven North nursing station. He could have been going through to Seven South with the pillows.

"Or he could've just been delivering linen to the South ward," said Moose. "When I get to work at six tomorrow morning, I'll talk to the nurses, get back to you."

Lenny thanked his friend and sipped his coffee. Birdie was puzzled about what she called the one 'big question': did the patient leave on her own or was she forced to go with the mystery man. Moose suggested that somebody could have brought the pillows in, kidnapped Bowen and taken her away, using the pillows to buy time before the empty bed was discovered.

Asked how Lenny knew that a man in surgical scrubs was seen on Seven North the night the patient disappeared, he told Stone he had watched the video recordings of the surveillance cameras covering both wards.

Stone was surprised that Lenny could access the video files, they were confidential, but he realized the wily shop steward had friends all over the hospital who would bend the rules for him. Lenny added that the video showed the missing woman did not walk past the Seven South nursing station, which is where the only video camera on the ward was placed. There were only two other ways of the ward: the stairwell at the far end of the hall, or crossing over to Seven North.

He explained that if Clair went out by the stairs, she would have avoided being seen by either of the video cameras on the two wards.

The physician looked at Moose, who grinned and said, "That's our boy."

Lenny hurriedly finished his coffee, he had an appointment in Human Resources, it was time to execute the second step grievance, having skipped the first step as a useless waste of time and energy. There was no way Boris Nasir would have listened to reason on the issue of family leave.

16

When Lenny stepped into the Human Resources office, the secretary pointed at the door to Mr. Freely's office, indicating the union man should go right in. He found the Director seated at his desk, sports coat off, lavender bow tie askew. Freely gestured for Lenny to take a seat, leaned forward and placed his elbows on the desk.

"No doubt you came to no agreement with Step One," said Freely.

Lenny pointed out that an informal discussion with the immediate supervisor was pointless, since he was just carrying out a directive from the president and had no authority to countermand it. That's why Lenny was starting with the second step.

Freely had a weary look on his face, like he hadn't slept much lately, or maybe his sleep was filled with bad dreams.

"Lenny, how many times have we met across my desk like this over the years?"

Taken aback by the question, Lenny settled into a chair and counted the number of years he'd been a steward. "Let's see, I've been a steward for, what, twelve years? If I had maybe twenty, twenty-five cases I needed to bring to your department every year, that makes it..."

"Too many and too much heartache." Freely sat back and looked up at the ceiling. "I want all our employees to have paid parental leave, regardless of their sexual orientation or lifestyle. You know that."

"I know what *you* want. That's not what President Reichart wants. Or allows."

Freely thanked Lenny for not using one of the numerous insulting phrases Lenny was known to employ when talking about the hated president of the hospital, like calling him "Third Reich Reichart" in a union flyer. The hedge fund manager had orchestrated the purchase of James

Madison Hospital a few years ago, and he immediately turned it from a non-profit institution to a highly profitable, highly controversial health care factory.

"You're gonna lose this one in arbitration," Lenny pointed out. "The law is clear and the prevailing sentiment is strong for LGBT rights, especially in Pennsylvania. The arbitrator will rule you have to pay both of the workers back wages with interest. And the public relations fallout is going to be a disaster if you don't give in on giving paid leave."

"I know, Lenny, I know. But I don't make the rules, I just try and make them work the best I can." Freely had a beleaguered, weary look on his face. The two had often argued, negotiated, traded insults and traded favors. The Director had always been fair in his dealings with the union. The problem was, the President was the iron fist inside Freely's velvet glove.

Lenny told him the campaign would get ugly. Gay rights organizations would jump on board, that would swell the demonstrations. City and commonwealth politicians will flock to the rallies.

Freely acknowledged all of it, but again he admitted his hands were tied. "Don't quote me to the press, Lenny, but do tell Missus Feekin and her family they have my deepest sympathy. When they win, I will be the first to congratulate them, but my orders come from on high."

"Or from down below, if you want to be more accurate in your geography."

Getting up to leave, Lenny told Freely he would speak to the union lawyer and see where they wanted to go. It would be a class action grievance at the least, or the union could go right to federal court and file a civil suit. Either way, they were bound to win in the end, it was the hospital dragging out a case that hurt the workers.

"You can expect informational picket lines next week," Lenny added from the doorway. "They'll be on the five o'clock news, and we won't be holding back our description of President Reichart."

17

Lenny sent a text message to all the union stewards, who passed on the news to the rank and file in their departments. Word spread quickly about Freely rejecting the step two grievance. Lenny also texted the union lawyer, David Rambling, expecting the counselor would want to meet with him soon to plan for Step Three, and he sent a short message to Margie with the bad news, asking her to be patient and let the union take the next step.

Regis was the first to reply to the text message: TIME TO HIT THE STREETS. Lenny broke out in a grin, pleased at how much the young man had learned about fighting for your rights. He'd come a long way from the hot-tempered fellow in the laundry who was always being written up. Now he was channeling his anger into union struggles, and he and the union were all the better for it.

The rest of the morning, Lenny answered questions from members and stewards. The workers were furious. They slammed the administration for playing it cheap and denying paid leave to anyone. Support was strong in every department. Lenny called for a stewards' meeting to plan how to support the grievance. He knew well the old military adage: *you win the war before going into battle.* Or as Rambling liked to say, *you fight in the streets to win in the courts.*

<>

At lunch time Lenny ate in the cafeteria so he could poll more workers about protesting the hospital's parental leave policy. Moose, Regis and Allison each sat down at a different table and talked up the issue. Support for Margie and Woody was strong. At Lenny's table, one worker from the laundry said, "I wish I could've stayed home with mine, but they were born a long time ago, we didn't have any paid leave for moms or dads back then."

"Would you stand on a picket line in front of the hospital?" Lenny asked, taking a bite out of a grilled chicken sandwich. "On your break time or your day off?"

"Name the day!" said a woman from Central Stores. "I'll bring my grandma, she loves a good fight! Mommy broke her hip a year ago last March, but soon as she was out of bed she was at the retiree meeting. With a walker!"

Lenny wiped some mayonnaise from his lips and smiled. Happy with the solidarity he was finding among his co-workers, he was about to get up and take his lunch to another table when Charity, an aide from the neonatal ICU came and sat down beside him.

"Lenny, you got a sec for me?"

"Sure, Charity, what's up? You in trouble?" He leaned close to the young woman so their conversation would not be overheard.

"No, I'm cool. It's just, I heard about the patient that disappeared two nights ago on your ward. Her name was Clair. Clair Bowen, right?"

"Yeah, that's right. What's it got to do with me?"

Charity rolled her eyes, she had no patience with Lenny's false modesty. "You probably already heard this, but Clair Bowen, used to work in the NICU. On the night shift. She quit after she got married. You do know who she was married to, don't you?"

"I don't know. Who?"

"She married that son of a bitch, Boris Nasir, one of the night supervisors. I don't know if it means anything, but I thought you oughta know."

Charity got up and went to sit with friends from the NICU at a little table on the side of the cafeteria.

Before returning to their wards, Lenny and the other union stewards huddled for a quick conference. They reported the same enthusiasm for the protest. "There's so much anger and frustration in the rank and file," Regis noted, "I think they'd go out and protest a change in the cafeteria menu."

Moose agreed, especially if the hospital stopped offering cow heel soup, it always sold out an hour after being put out in the big cafeteria soup buckets.

The anger had been building for a long time, starting when the Croesus hedge fund group bought the hospital, turned it private and then refused to honor the existing union contract. It had been downhill ever since. "When's the demonstration starting?" Moose asked. Lenny suggested they hold it the day of the Step Three grievance hearing.

"Soon as the union signs off on the date of the grievance hearing, I'll let everyone know," said Lenny. "Meantime, spread the word, we're going to raise holy hell."

Regis asked, "How many delegates you want us to bring to the hearing?

"I'd be happy to bring everybody on the street in to the meeting," Lenny said, referring to the old union strategy to "always bring a crowd." But for this one, he suggested that they cap the number of delegates at ten: enough of a show of force for the three vice presidents hearing the case to see the union had the overwhelming support of the membership, but not enough to give them an excuse to cancel the meeting.

Even if only one delegate got to argue the case before the bullshit tribunal, the line of delegates, each one able to bring twenty workers or more if needed, would get the message across.

For the first time in weeks, Lenny felt relaxed and calm. They had a battle plan. They had a strategy. They had the workers on their side.

He just wished he had someone on his side in the missing patient problem, especially with this new little gem of information: Clair Bowen married to that bastard Nasir.

What sense did that make, and what, if anything, could it have to do with her disappearance?

Then he remembered a friend in Employee Health he had helped in a big way some years back. He was just the person who could help him learn more about Clair Bowen-Nasir.

18

As soon as he returned to his ward, Lenny found his partner Mary in the little Seven South kitchen. "Mary, thanks so much for covering for me, I couldn't do what I so without you. Really I couldn't."

"Ain't no big thing," she said, peeling a hardboiled egg and tossing the shells in the little kitchen trash

"What's left to do?"

Mary told him she'd emptied all the trash liners, did a dry sweep of the hallway and took care of the staff bathroom. Only thing left was to take the rolling trash bucket down to the loading dock and empty it.

"That's good, I need to run by employee health, it's not far from the dock. Be back as quick as I can."

He pushed the big covered barrel down to the service elevator and rode it to the ground floor. From there he pushed it down to the loading dock, where Central Stores received their supplies and the city sanitation service picked up the trash. The medical waste was collected by a private agency and taken to a high-intensity incinerator for destruction of any potential pathogens.

Leaving the barrel inside the big double doors, Lenny hurried along the corridor and turned to the wing where Employee Health Services was located.

Lenny waved to Mandy at the Employee Health reception desk. "How ya doin' today?" he asked.

"Ah, that husband of mine is *still* driving me to drink," she said, shaking her head. Mandy was a white-haired nurse with swollen ankles and puffy eyes who had just one more year to work until retirement. "He keeps telling me I need to lose forty pounds on account of my sugar is up."

"He loves you, that ain't bad."

"*Love? Hah!* He's just irritated because I wake him up two, three times a night

when I get out of bed to go pee."

"You could sleep in separate beds."

"Nah. We've been sleeping butt to butt for so long, my ass would catch cold without him beside me."

"Yeah, I see what you mean. Listen, any chance Doctor Primeaux is free?"

"Got a drip again, Lenny?" she asked with a smirk, teasing that he might be suffering from a venereal disease that caused a purulent discharge from his penis. Mandy well knew that Lenny was a solid family man, to the disappointment of not a few women workers around the facility.

She gave Lenny a gesture with her thumb, meaning he could go on down to the Employee Health doctor's office. With a single knock, he entered the little office, where he found Alex Primeaux's desk piled high with employee charts, an old stethoscope nestled on top and a glass bowl with chocolate candies beside it.

"How are things in your world, Lenny?" the doctor asked.

Lenny closed the door, indicating this would be a private conversation. "Oh, same old same old. Reichart wants to kill our pension and steal our wages. The usual stuff."

Primeaux was deeply sympathetic. He knew that stress on the job made workers sicker, made them die younger, and impaired the quality of their work. How could you be always cheerful with your patient when you were stuck in mandatory overtime, and working short staffed at that?

"This one's a bit delicate," Lenny offered. He and the Employee Health doctor had worked together on a case years ago. In the course of the investigation Lenny had learned a dangerous secret about the good doctor; a secret the wily shop steward promised to keep, which he faithfully had done. Doctor Primeaux was grateful for Lenny keeping his promise of silence and would help him with any favor, even if it was outside the hospital rules. Or the law.

"I'm trying to help a nurse on the night shift, she's being terminated over that patient that disappeared last week."

"Catherine Feekin," the doctor said. "I heard about that. Terrible thing to blame a nurse when a patient elopes. Terrible."

"It turns out the patient in question was a nurse by the name of Clair Bowen. She worked here in the NICU until she got married. I need to know everything you can tell me about her. Like, today."

Dr. Primeaux looked at his hands: they were sensitive instruments that felt for lesions, fractures, pockets of infection. Hands that healed. Hands he washed or sanitized a hundred times a day.

"Lenny, I can't give out the employee files. Not even for you. But I know Clair Bowen.... I know her too well. She had a troubled life, starting in childhood. Abusive father, abusive boyfriends. She went to nursing school to get her independence, but in the end, she married an abusive man."

"Boris Nasir."

"Boris Nasir. She was out of work three times in two years for 'illness.' Except it wasn't the flu or chronic back pain, it was for rib fractures. Facial contusions. One time she came in with hematuria. Blood in the urine. She tried to attribute it to a urinary tract infection, but I suspected it was from a beating."

"Kidney punch," said Lenny. "It's easy to hide, doesn't always leave a mark on the skin."

"That's what I thought. When she was due for her annual health assessment, I tried to convince her to see a counselor. A priest. *Somebody*. But I think she was just too scared to break away. She quit her job at the hospital not long after her last visit to Employee Health."

Lenny asked if he would check to see if she'd been treated at the hospital after she left the job. Primeaux called up the patient's medical records. He identified three visits to the Emergency Room, though she had never been admitted. She was treated again for blood in the urine, and once for bruising to the cervical spine.

Lenny told him he'd seen all too many women stay with abusive partners. He talked about the young woman in the laundry who came to work one day wearing sunglasses and heavy makeup. Lenny knew right away she had been slapped around.

"I tried to talk to her, but she wouldn't let me bring it up. Lucky for her, the laundry supervisor was sympathetic. She agreed to holding a mandatory in-service for all the laundry workers on spouse abuse, with one of the social workers leading the program. In the meeting the girl broke down and told her story. It was the first step."

"To freedom. Seems to me you had something to do with that in-service."

Lenny shrugged, not wanting to take the credit.

"Wait a sec," said Lenny, "you said Clair hadn't been admitted for her last ER visits. What about her admission last week? The one where she disappeared?"

The doctor noted that up until last week, Clair Bowen had always given her married name to the clerk. This last visit was the first time she'd gone back to her maiden name.

Lenny told the doctor that the ER doctor was puzzled by the case because her blood count was normal even though she vomited up a lot of blood. At first he thought she had a GI bleed from taking a lot of aspirin, but then with the normal count, he chalked it up to a nosebleed that she swallowed.

Asked what he made of the case, Primeaux agreed, it was puzzling. He opened up her employee health record looking for a history of bleeding, but found none. "Huh, this is odd," he said. "Clair Bowen had an allergy to aspirin. Actually, a sensitivity due to tinnitus, but it amounts to the same thing. She wouldn't have been taking it for any reason."

"So aspirin didn't have anything to do with her bleeding," said Lenny.

"That's right."

Lenny tucked the information away in his mind. It was one more piece of a puzzle that was getting more and more obscure.

As Lenny got up to leave, Dr. Primeaux asked him if he thought Clair's husband killed her. He hoped in his heart that Clair had not paid the ultimate price, as he knew too many abuse victims had done.

"I'm hoping she's alive and in hiding," said Lenny. "The fact that she used her maiden name in the ER makes me think she was trying to hide from her husband." He didn't mention the mystery man with the limp who'd appeared in the surveillance video, there was no need to burden the doctor with that.

"I certainly hope so. Clair Bowen lived to care for others, but she never took care of herself. She deserves better."

"Hmm." Lenny wondered aloud if Nasir had filed a missing person's report. He had a contact in the police department. Much as it sometimes created as many problems as it solved, he decided it was time to talk to a certain detective he had worked with on past cases.

The man was a homicide detective. Lenny hoped this time the police would not have to make that kind of investigation.

19

On his way to the Housekeeping office to punch out, Lenny ran into Moose, who was cleaning one of the big rolling carts that carried the food trays to the wards. Moose reminded Lenny they were scheduled to go jogging in Fairmont Park Saturday morning.

"Aw, I don't know, Moose, I'm dead tired, it's been a hell of a week."

"That's all the more reason to go for a run, it'll rejuvenate you."

"More like put me in an early grave." He told his friend about Malcolm wanting to play junior football. Moose, who had been a completive boxer in high school, suggested martial arts. "It gives a kid confidence and strength, and there's no chance him getting hit in the head."

"I'm afraid Patience would hit *me* in the head if I suggested karate."

Spraying more cleaner on the inside of the cart, Moose ran a rag over the steel wall. He pointed out that soccer was getting more and more popular in the US. "Look at the women's World Cup. Man, the media coverage was off the charts."

"You're suggesting Malcolm play on the girl's soccer team?"

Moose ignored the crack. "It's a clean sport, super aerobic. You could coach him, those city teams are always looking for parents to help out."

Lenny had to admit, it was a tempting idea. "Malcolm would get plenty of exercise, and we would spend Saturday mornings together when it was my weekend off. And the best thing about it? You'd have to stop nagging me about going jogging!"

Moose turned his attention back to the cleaning job, while Lenny, pleased with his latest excuse for avoiding exercise with his friend, went to the office to punch out.

<>

Over dinner, Lenny told Patience and Malcolm about Moose's suggestion that they enroll the lad in a soccer team. Lenny even offered to coach the team on the Saturdays that he was off. Malcolm wasn't interested, he'd never played soccer, and Patience was concerned that they hit the ball with their head.

"I don't see why the soccer players don't sustain brain injuries just like football players," she said.

Lenny promised he would do some research and find out if young or adult soccer players developed any of the brain damage symptoms that football players did. While Malcolm still showed no enthusiasm, Lenny pointed out he didn't have to stick with it if he didn't like it. "Besides," he added, "It'll be fun being on a team. You'll make a lot of friends, and after every game the coach takes everyone out for ice cream."

"They do?" said Malcolm, brightening a bit.

"Sure. And I'll be with you the whole time, it'll be great!"

"O-kay, I'll try it one time. But if I don't like it I don't have t' go back."

Lenny agreed, there was no commitment, it was an experiment. When Malcolm got up to bus his plate and start washing the dishes — the children took turns with that task — Patience leaned over and whispered to Lenny, "Ice cream after the game? You made that up, didn't you?"

Lenny soaked up the last of the gravy on his plate with a piece of bread and reminded his wife that he had an important meeting scheduled for after dinner.

<>

90

After dinner, Patience helped the children with their homework, Takia never complaining about the work, Malcolm always moaning and groaning. Lenny looked at his watch, saw his appointment was due any minute.

"You might set out some whiskey and mixer," his wife suggested, knowing the visitor enjoyed Lenny's Evan Williams bourbon as much as her husband did. Plus, there was nothing like a little liquor to loosen a tongue.

Lenny fetched the bottle, glasses and seltzer. He had just put down the tray when he heard a loud knock, knock, knock on the door. Opening the door onto the porch, he saw the tall, intimidating figure standing there in silhouette, right out of aa 1940's movie.

Detective Joe Williams was a big man who could intimidate a suspect or witness. The police officer had dealt with Lenny on numerous murder cases. The first few times their interactions had been strained and antagonistic. There had been no trust between them. But over time each had learned to trust the other man...within limits. Williams understood Lenny had access to people and areas of the hospital he could not reach, and Lenny knew that the police had information gathering capabilities that were out of his league.

"Detective Williams. Nice of you to drop by."

"I've got a full plate these days, Lenny, this better be good." Williams had a sour look on his face. His usually neatly pressed suit was wrinkled, his signature handkerchief in the breast pocket missing.

Lenny ushered the detective into the living room and gestured for him to take a seat. When Williams saw the bottle of bourbon, his mood lightened.

"Make mine a double, two rocks," he said.

Lenny gave them both a healthy pour. Once they were settled with their drinks, Lenny got down to business. He explained he was investigating the disappearance of a patient from the hospital in the middle of Wednesday night. Maybe she eloped, maybe she was abducted...or worse.

He added that the picture was confusing, the woman came in with signs of a bleeding stomach ulcer, but the ER doctor wasn't sure about the diagnosis, and the patient apparently lied about taking aspirin, which she was allergic to. Plus, there was no sign of a GI bleed in the room: no dirty towels, no stains in the toilet, and her personal belongings were still in the room.

"You think she left against her will?"

"There's no way to know. But I can tell you she was married to a first-class son of a bitch, a night shift Housekeeping supervisor name of Ralph Nasir." Lenny told Williams about the video recording from that night that showed a man with a limp in surgical scrubs who might not belong on the ward. And with no sight of the woman passing the surveillance cameras at the two nursing stations, the only way for her to leave was by the stairwell.

Williams said, "Listen, Lenny, let's stop the dancing around and cut to the chase. What do you want the police to do?"

"I'll tell you, even though your mixed metaphors are gruesome." Getting not the hint of a smile out of Williams, Lenny asked the detective to find out if the husband, Ralph Nasir, had filed a missing person's report.

The detective looked over his glass with the beginning of interest. "The husband should have filed the report, assuming she is actually missing. If he didn't file the report, why not? Do you know that the wife is actually not at home?"

Lenny said the hospital's patient advocate had called multiple times, it was hospital practice when a patient went missing. They even asked the local precinct to send an officer to knock on her door: nobody home.

Williams promised to check on the report and get back to him the next day. Then he told Lenny that the wily steward had to pass on any new information or insight he had on the missing woman. Lenny agreed, so long as the detective shared his information as well.

"Maybe you could do a background check on her," Lenny said. "I'd like to know as much about her as I can. Does she have connections to any illegal activities? Arrest for drug possession? Anything and everything you can give me."

"Don't push your luck, Moss." Williams set down his empty glass. "I'll do what I can, so long as it's a two-way street."

20

On Saturday Lenny phoned Moose to tell him he was taking Malcolm to try out for the local soccer team. His friend protested it was a lame excuse for not going jogging, but Lenny countered that he would be getting lots of exercise running with the children. "We'll do wind sprints, I'll be right behind them on the field, it'll be great."

Moose knew better, but let it slide.

Lenny walked with Malcolm to the local city field, where the soccer team was meeting. His arm around Malcolm's shoulder, Lenny introduced his son to the coach. He was about to ask what were the requirements for trying out, when he stopped. "Hey, you're Joe Doc, aren't you? We were in the same elementary school, weren't we? Pennypacker, right?"

"That's right. Oh, yeah, you're Lenny. Lenny Moss. Sure, you were a grade behind me. Man, that was, what, thirty years ago?"

"Feels more like a hundred. Hey, it's good to see you again."

They soon sorted out the application process. Lenny signed a permission slip and promised that Malcolm was not allergic to peanuts or had a congenital heart condition. Joe dropped a soccer ball on the ground and suggested Malcolm join a line of boys who were to kick the ball to the coach and trap it when he returned it.

As the couch called all the boys together for a pep talk, Moose walked up to Lenny and sat beside him on the grass. "I don't see you doin' no wind sprints," Moose said.

"We did them at the start of practice, you missed it."

"Heh, heh. Don't think you're getting off easy, we still got Sunday to go for that run."

"I'll be in church."

"You're Jewish."

"I'm an atheist, but thanks for acknowledging my roots."

As they watched the children get back to kicking the ball, Lenny told Moose what he'd learned about Clair Bowen: that she had been married to Nasir, that she'd suffered abuse at his hands, and that she'd been to the ER a number of times with suspicious injuries after she stopped working at James Madison.

"You gotta think Nasir had something to do with his wife going up in smoke," said Moose. "I've heard stories from people on the graveyard shift about him taking advantage of the young women working nights. They're scared to speak up, 'fraid they'll lose their job. He's about as evil as they come."

"I'm sure President Reichart is thrilled to have him on staff."

Moose grimaced when a child tried to give the ball a good kick and ended up on his backside, legs up in the air. "You're gonna keep digging, aren't you?"

Lenny waved to Malcolm, who dribbled and then passed the ball to a team mate. "I don't know, I've got my hands full with this class action grievance. We're going to have to build for support from the community for a big demonstration — that's a shitload of work."

"Yeah, but the woman disappeared on your floor. It's one of your nurses in trouble."

"She's not in our union, Moose, she's not in *any* union."

"That's why you have to help her. There's nobody else can do it."

Lenny turned his attention back to the children, many of whom seemed to not know where they were supposed to be positioned or how they could function as a team. "Jesus H. Christ. What do I need to know to help coach the team? You ever play soccer?"

Moose clapped his friend on the shoulder. "All you need to know is, keep your hands away from the ball and try to remember who's on your team and who's on the other."

"Nice play, Malcolm!" Lenny called when the boy took a shot at the net, missing and sending the ball high over the net, but happy to have sent the ball soaring into the air. He looked over at Lenny, who gave the boy a thumbs up and a look of encouragement.

"What're you gonna do next?" Moose asked.

Lenny turned to his friend. "I asked that detective, Joe Williams, to find out if Nasir filed a missing persons report on his wife. If he didn't, it makes me think the bastard knows where his wife is...his dead and buried wife."

A girl on the opposing team dribbled the ball toward the goal, showing outstanding footwork. Malcolm tried to keep up with her, but she was fast. The girl gave the ball a kick. It bounced off the goal keeper's arm and slipped into the net. Parents for the team stood up and cheered.

Malcolm watched the girl who'd scored with his mouth and eyes wide open.

"Looks like your boy's in love," Moose said, pointing at Malcolm.

"Great, that's all I need. Now he'll *never* do his homework."

<>

On the way home from soccer practice Lenny stopped for ice cream, since Malcolm pointed out he had promised the coach took the team out after practice. When they finally got home, Patience saw the chocolate ice cream on her son's face and sent him upstairs for a bubble bath. She suggested that Lenny stretch out in the hot water when her son was finished. "It's a good stress release, Lenny," she told him. "Do you good."

While Malcolm was soaking, Lenny told Patience about the game. He confirmed that he'd asked the coach if he could help out on his weekends off, an offer that was gladly accepted. The coach knew he had never played the game and knew next to nothing about it, but at the age of these kids it was all about going out on the field and having fun. Sometimes nobody even scored a goal.

He checked his cell phone, having turned it off while out with Malcolm. There were several messages from his fellow stewards asking when was the next step in the grievance was going to be. He sent a reply to all of them saying he had to speak to their lawyer Rambler in the union office and would let them know as soon as he had a date and time. Meantime, they needed to build for a demonstration in front of the hospital: an all -out, big and loud protest that got them media time and scared the crap out of the assholes in the administrative wing.

When Malcolm came downstairs in sweatpants and sweatshirt, Lenny took his own turn in the bath. Settling into the still-warm water, he smiled to remember the first time he'd helped Malcolm in the tub. The boy was still playing with tub toys, something Lenny enjoyed as much as he did. Who doesn't love a rubber ducky?

While he tried to focus on the case he was bringing for LGBT rights, his mind kept wandering to the mystery of the disappearing patient. Had she walked out on her own steam, been abducted or murdered? By a stranger? By her husband? And if a crime was committed, why? Why attack a shy young woman?

His glanced around the room and saw some of the children's makeup Patience had bought for their upcoming Halloween costumes. Trick or treat was second only to Christmas in their ranking of favorite holidays, they picked up so much candy, to his wife's great chagrin and repeated complaints.

Takia wanted to dress up like one of the Supremes, complete with wig, fake eye lashes and high heels. Patience thought it was a terrible idea to present herself as a sex object at her age of twelve. Malcolm wanted to go as a vampire, with lots of fake blood running down his face. He wanted the fake teeth, too, so he could pretend to bite people on the neck, something he enjoyed with peals of laughter and a big grin on his—.

"Holy shit!"

Lenny sat up in his chair as the idea hit him like a line-backer ready to take the head off of a running back coming through the line. *What if Clair Bowen's GI bleed wasn't a bleed after all? What if she faked all of her symptoms?*

It made sense of the way she had left the bathroom: no evidence of bloody diarrhea, no sign of washing up after a bowel movement or after throwing up.

There was no evidence of an actual Gi bleed at all.

Lenny concluded that if Clair Bowen faked her illness, that was evidence that she had left the hospital voluntarily. Which begged the question of why? But Lenny was confident that the answer would come out, it was only a matter of digging and digging until the truth came out.

<>

Dressed in sweat pants and sweatshirt like his son, Lenny went into the kitchen to make supper. He announced me was making his favorite: grilled cheese sandwiches and tomato soup. Patience agreed, but insisted she would make a salad, knowing how much fat her husband put in all the meals he cooked.

Sure enough, Lenny spread butter on the outside *and* inside of the bread. He sautéed bacon on a cast iron skillet, poured the fat into a saucepan and emptied two cans of tomato soup into it. Then he gently heated the soup, stirring in a bit of cream and a generous shake of hot sauce.

He layered the bacon and cheese slices in the sandwiches and cooked them in the pan still wet with bacon fat. The sweet smell of bacon and cheese wafted out of the kitchen, bringing smiles to the faces of the children and a look of anguish on his wife's.

Patience made Malcolm eat salad first, not even trying to serve greens to Lenny, who pointed out that tomato soup was made from...tomatoes, a vegetable. Patience didn't bother correcting him that tomatoes were a fruit.

21

Monday morning dawned brisk and breezy, with leaves beginning to fall and a threat of rain in the air. Lenny's partner Little Mary hadn't been pulled to another ward, miracle of miracles, so he had a shot at a "normal" workday for a change.

Lenny began his shift collecting the trash liners from the patient rooms, the weekend staff was always a skeleton crew who left much of the work for the weekday staff He was rolling the big trash barrel down the hall, throwing tied off trash liners in and stretching new ones in the plastic buckets, when Margie came marching up to him.

"Yo, Lenny! You're not gonna believe what that rotten bastard Nasir has done to me!"

"Calm down, Margie, please. Take a deep breath and just fill me in."

After slowing down her breathing, Margie explained that the minute she punched in at eleven o'clock, Nasir handed her a notice of suspension. She showed it to Lenny, who saw that the administration alleged Margie had made threats of violence against supervisor Boris Nasir. She was suspended with the intention of eventual termination.

"You didn't stay in the hospital all night, did you?"

"Nah, I caught a few z's in my car out in the lot. I had to wait for you to come on duty. But listen: they can't get away with this shit, can they? Can they just fire my ass for running my big mouth? I didn't mean what I said, I was just blowin' smoke is all."

Lenny told her the first thing she needed to do was stop talking to anyone from work about the suspension. He repeated the advice he'd give many a worker when they were in trouble: "Nobody talks, everyone walks." He asked what exactly had she said, where had she said it and who did she say it to.

Margie admitted she had blown off a little steam a couple of nights ago at the start of her shift. She was talking with Louisa.

"Was anyone else there?"

"Catherine came up. She heard some of it."

"Shit. That means the dispatcher heard it, too. If he signs a statement, it'll be hard to fight it, but I'll give it my best shot." He told her to go home, get some sleep and wait to hear from him, and not talk to anyone from work about the incident.

Before leaving, Margie asked what day and time was the union setting up the demonstration. She swore she was ready to shut the whole fricking place down.

<>

As soon as Margie left, Lenny hurried down to the Housekeeping department hoping to catch hold of Nasir. The steward didn't expect to be able to talk the cold-hearted supervisor into changing his mind on the suspension, but the union contract called for a first step informal talk with the supervisor if it was at all possible to settle the issue at a local departmental level.

In the department he found Childress, the Housekeeping Director, talking with Manny, one of the day supervisors. Asked if Nasir was still around, Childress told him he hadn't seen him that morning.

"Did he leave early or what?" Lenny asked. Manny volunteered that Nasir's jacket and briefcase were still in the office, so he was probably having breakfast.

Lenny asked the office secretary to page Nasir STAT, but when she did, the secretary got no answer to her page. He didn't answer on his walkie-talkie, either. Frustrated and seriously pissed off, Lenny told the director he'd have a grievance filed by the end of the day, and walked out of the department.

<>

After returning to the ward and catching up with his housekeeping duties, Lenny called Dr. Stone in the ER, relieved to learn that the doctor was on duty. "Listen, doc, I've got an off-the-wall question about Clair Bowen for you: could she have faked her gastric ulcer disease?"

"What brings you to that conclusion?" the doctor asked.

"For one thing, she told you in the ER she had been taking aspirin for a sore knee, but Employee Health tells me she was allergic to aspirin."

"That is quite interesting."

"And the way her room looked in the morning, no bloody stool, no sign she washed up, you know how messy GI bleeders are. The whole thing could have been a ruse to get her in the hospital."

Stone was silent for a few seconds before saying, "That explains a lot of what's been puzzling me." He told Lenny he'd been struck by the symptoms that Clair presented with, they didn't sync with her lab work, but he couldn't figure out why.

"What about the blood? Could she have, like, swallowed blood?"

"Sure. It would take a lot of guts, but, yeah, people have been drinking the blood of their enemies for centuries, there's no contraindication there."

When Lenny asked about the black stools that Clair had reported, Stone said that would be easy to fake as well. If she had started swallowing blood two or three days before, that would darken the stool. Or she could have taken activated charcoal, a medication they used to draw off drugs in an overdose case. Easy to buy over the counter, and it darkens the stool as much as blood does.

103

Lenny was beginning to think that Clair had had friends to help her in the entire episode. Somebody would have to give her the blood, that meant a friend in the Blood Bank.

Then he realized that she must have had a friend helping to not just get admitted with the fake bleed, but also, to escape sight unseen.

22

Regis Devoe set the scalpels and saws out to be ready for the first autopsy of the day. He recalled a section in the text book he'd been studying about the dangers of cross-contamination of bodies when an infectious process was being considered in the diagnosis. Although the pathologist did not have to be concerned with causing an infection by transferring pathogens from one cadaver to another, as happened when caring for living patients, it was still important to not produce false culture reports when collecting specimens from a dead body's blood and tissue.

The young assistant took satisfaction recalling his first time helping Dr. Fingers with an autopsy. The pathologist had asked if Regis was bothered by the sight of a scalpel cutting into a body. Regis had told him no, he wasn't, the person's suffering was behind him, he was in a better place, god willing.

"Amen to that," Fingers had replied, finding satisfaction in hiring Regis based on Lenny's recommendation. It had been a good choice, the young man was working out well.

Walking down the hall to the big cold locker where they stored cadavers, Regis opened the door and squeezed his way between the stretchers. He lifted the sheet on one body, read the toe tag and went on to the next. When he lifted the sheet, he was startled to find shiny black shoes and black socks on the body's feet. In fact, the body was fully clothed. That was not hospital protocol, all bodies going to the morgue had to be naked and tagged. Period, no exceptions.

Pulling back the sheet, Regis found himself looking at a middle-aged male, white, with thinning gray hair combed across the top of his head, thin lips and a deformity on the left side of the head: the parietal region. Regis was confident Dr. Fingers would identify a depressed skull fracture. There was little or no swelling or mottling at the site, which told him death had been rapid, almost instantaneous: a fatal blow that left no time for blood to collect beneath the skin.

Turning to leave the cold locker, Regis stopped, turned back and looked one more time at the face of the dead man. Although he had never worked the midnight shift when he'd been assigned to the laundry, Regis had heard enough complaints from the laundry workers on the graveyard shift to know which supervisor was the biggest pain in the ass. The night crew had filed many a complaint against that hated man. Regis had occasionally seen him in the morning chewing out a worker and filing disciplinary actions.

Leaving the locker, Regis took out his cell phone. He knew his first responsibility was to call his supervisor, Dr. Fingers. But before he made that call, he pressed the speed button to call Lenny Moss and tell him that Boris Nasir was dead.

23

Lenny was getting into the rhythm of his day. He'd put a new pad on the buffer and was polishing the old marble floor. Though it was cracked in places and needed to be replaced, he was still able to put a shine on the surface that would last a few hours.

He was moving the buffer side to side in broad arcs, letting the rhythmic sound blur out the noise in the hall and giving him time to think. He needed to talk to a few other stewards about meeting to plan for the Step Three grievance — the one they had a shot at winning if they brought enough pressure to bear on the bosses.

All of a sudden, somebody tapped him on the shoulder. He switched off the machine, turned around and saw Detective Joe Williams standing in the middle of the hall.

"Morning, Lenny. Have any news for me?"

"Damn, I thought you were gonna bring the news to *me.*" When Williams kept silent, with a poker face, Lenny suggested they step into his office, there was no privacy in the hall.

He led the detective to the housekeeping locker, telling Mary he would be in conference for a bit. She waved with a grin and promised to cover for him.

Lenny turned two empty plastic buckets over and settled onto one, saying, "How's about you start. Did Nasir file a missing person report on his wife or not?"

"No."

Lenny studied the detective's face. He realized, as he had with numerous other interactions with Williams, that the man was as good at putting on a poker face, or an innocent face, or a challenging face as he was. Lenny wondered if Williams was as good at arching a single eyebrow, but decided not to challenge him on it.

"You did talk to the bastard, didn't you?"

Williams took out a pocket notebook and thumbed through it. Lenny asked why didn't he switch to a digital notebook, they were living in a digital age, but the detective ignored the wisecrack.

Williams confirmed he'd interviewed Nasir at his home Saturday afternoon, waking him up, apparently. The man claimed he hadn't been aware of his wife's admission to the hospital on Wednesday night until the night nurse reported her missing. When he heard the name, Clair Bowen, he of course realized who it was. When he arrived home Thursday morning, she was gone, leaving no note, no email message. No word on where she'd gone, or why.

"And he didn't wonder what happened? He didn't care if she was out in the street someplace bleeding to death?"

"He said his wife had been unhappy all her life. A 'miserable, whining little you know what' were how he described her. He figured she'd run off to stay with a girl friend and would, as he said, 'crawl back when she was ready.' I didn't believe anything he said."

"You gotta think he killed her, it's the only logical conclusion. I mean, when he learned that a 'Clair Bowen' had eloped, he didn't bother to tell anyone it was his *wife* who'd gone up in smoke."

"I agree, it's suspicious. He could have learned she was admitted somehow. But how did he get her body out of the hospital? I reviewed all the video surveillance recordings, there was no body carried off the ward or out of the facility."

"Actually, there was," said Lenny. "Follow me, I'll show you."

Lenny led the detective to the stairwell near the end of the ward, just shy of the passage to Seven North. Opening the door to the stairs, he said, "This is where Clair made her escape." They walked down to the ground floor,

Lenny's steel-tipped work shoes thudding on the metal steps as they descended to the first floor. On the landing they came upon an exit with a big sign in bold red letters: WARNING! EMERGENCY EXIT ONLY – ALARM WILL SOUND IF OPENED!

In the most casual motion imaginable, Lenny depressed the bar on the door, pushed on it and opened the door.

No alarm.

"Somebody — and I honestly don't know who — disabled the alarm so they could come and go on their own time. See the cigarette butts on the ground? Some guys step out for a smoke, some go out for a drink or to meet a friend. It's a pretty common practice."

Williams made a call for a forensics team to examine the door for fingerprints, though he admitted that would be a one-in-a-million chance, but better not to leave the stone unturned. Then he asked what else had he learned. Lenny told him he had evidence Clair had been abused by her husband, describing his interview with Dr. Primeaux in Employee Health. She had resisted the doctor's requests that she see a therapist or get help in any way.

"That's a common habit with abuse victims," said Williams.

"So I understand. There's one more wrinkle to Clair's hospital admission: I have a hunch she wasn't bleeding from her stomach at all." He explained that Clair could have swallowed blood and then vomited it back up in the ER. From what the doctor in the Emergency Room told him, the blood she vomited was pretty dramatic.

"You'd have to be awfully desperate to swallow a bucket of blood," said Williams.

"Well, she was a woman abused. Desperate times..."

Williams chewed on the new idea, then asked why would a woman fake an illness that serious? Lenny told him Clair had been abused for years, maybe she had a friend in the hospital who was helping her get out. Get away to safety.

The detective didn't comment. He didn't even make an entry in his little notebook. Lenny couldn't tell if Williams thought the idea was too stupid to consider or too important to forget.

He was asking Williams if the police had found any history of drug abuse in Clair's past when the chirp of his cell phone halted Lenny in mid-sentence. He'd set different ring tones for different people, and Regis, as an active shop steward, had his own sound.

"Yeah, Re'ege... Uh-huh...I see... Okay, got it.... No, you don't have to call the police, I'll do that for you, you just let Doctor Fingers know...Yes, I'm sure, it's no problem at all. I'll be down there soon as I can."

Putting away his phone, Lenny showed Williams his best, most practiced deadpan, give-nothing-away look. Speaking in a flat voice, he said, "You might want to join me at the morgue and check out one of the corpses, the cold locker is one flight down in the basement. The morgue attendant, Regis Devoe, has something to show you."

"Oh?" said Williams. "Don't tell me they found the missing woman."

"Afraid not. But they did find a body in the cold storage locker that didn't belong there. It's the night supervisor for Housekeeping, Ralph Nasir."

24

When Lenny called Mary and told her he had to go to the morgue and would be back as soon as he could, she asked what kind of union business did he have down there? He told her a supervisor had left work kind of suddenly, it had all sorts of implications for the workers he'd been jerking around.

He led Williams to the morgue, where Dr. Fingers, a security guard and a member of the hospital's Rick Management Office were standing outside the cold storage locker. When the Rick Management officer tried to tell Lenny to go back to his unit, the 'incident' had nothing to do with union business, this was a matter for the police, Williams flashed his Philadelphia detective badge and ordered the man to open the locker.

The detective gestured for the physician to enter the locker first, then he stepped inside, with Lenny close behind him. Before the hospital boss could utter an objection, Williams gave him a hard stare. The detective knew that what Lenny lacked in formal forensic training he more than made up for it with his understanding of hospital workings.

"Don't they keep the bodies under lock and key?" Williams asked. Dr. Fingers explained that ever since a hospital employee had been trapped inside due to an unforeseen danger, they had eliminated the lock. Neither Fingers nor Lenny bothered to tell the detective it had been Lenny trapped in the locker and nearly dying from hypothermia.

Fingers pulled back the sheet. Nasir was lying on his back, fully clothed, as Regis had reported. His eyes were half open, giving the creepy illusion that he was watching them stand around. Lenny didn't like it, but he'd helped

Regis, and Freddie the former morgue attendant, cart away enough bodies to be used to it.

Lenny confirmed the man's identity. The detective found the man's wallet, examined the driver's license and had no doubt as to the identity of the victim.

"Blunt force trauma," Williams noted, turning the head and bending down to get a good look at the head wound.

"A fatal blow, I think," Fingers added, admitting he would need a formal autopsy to confirm his finding. "It will be difficult to determine the time of death accurately, the body is fully chilled."

Lenny told Williams he had looked for Nasir at the start of his shift, but the man had not been seen in at least a few hours. The detective instructed Fingers to keep the body where it was and to keep the security guard there to prevent anyone entering the cold locker. He had to report the body to his department and wait for instructions.

After promising Williams that he would do what he could to find out more about Nasir's midnight shift, Lenny left to return to the ward, intending to find out as much as he could about Nasir's movements during the night. Riding the elevator up to the seventh floor, he had one thought weighing on his mind that was going to be one hell of a headache: Margie had told him she spent the night in her car in the hospital parking lot.

What was there to prevent her from slipping into the hospital by that emergency exit with the disabled alarm and doing away with that rat bastard Ralph Nasir?

25

Lenny returned to his ward, troubled by Nasir's death. Williams hadn't suggested he had the names of any suspects in the bastard's death, but it wouldn't take the detective long to learn Nasir had made a fistful of enemies on the night shift. And number one on that list was sure to be his friend, the high-strung housekeeper with serious anger management issues, Margie Aquinos. As if being suspended wasn't bad enough.

Lenny wished he didn't have to stick his big nose into other people's troubles. But years ago he'd volunteered for the steward job, it was what he did, what he was, he was too old to change, and if defending a worker for a murder charge was a bit out of the normal steward's handbook, he would just have to walk down that road. Besides, kicking the bosses in the ass was the best part of life, why give it up now?

He texted Regis and asked his friend to get as much information he could from Doctor Fingers about how and when Nasir was killed. If they were supremely lucky, the Medical Examiner would let Fingers perform the autopsy, they often outsourced the work to James Madison, the hospital did it for free to give house staff and students experience cutting up a corpse.

Resuming his housekeeping duties, he turned his attention to the parental leave grievance. Since the second step meeting with Mr. Freely in Human Resources had been a bust, his next move was to go over the grievance with the union lawyer, Dave Rambling. Rambling promised to meet him for lunch, but they needed a private spot, so they agreed to take lunch in the sewing room.

Since Lenny wanted to bring in a couple of the younger stewards to give them experience in going through the grievance process, he asked Regis Devoe to join them. Regis covered pathology and all the labs, including the phlebotomy team, so he had a substantial area to cover. Moose from Dietary and Allison, who covered the nurse aides and ward clerks, came too, and he sent a text message to Woody, since he was named in the grievance.

Grabbing his habitual donut and coffee, Lenny hurried down to the sewing room. He found Woody there chatting away with Birdie. So were Regis, Allison and Moose. A moment later the union lawyer knocked and entered.

Rambler was a tall, lanky fellow from North Carolina. He brought a lazy cadence in his talk that gave his opponent in court the impression that he wasn't fast on his feet. Wrong assessment. He had a quicksilver mind and a sharp tongue when he needed it, and he knew the labor case law like nobody else.

Taking a seat in the sewing room, Rambler began, "The way I see it, we have two choices. We can file a civil suit in federal court and argue the hospital is denying the two workers, and all workers who may fall into their protected status, equal protection under the law that forbids discrimination based on sex or sexual orientation." He added that federal cases took a long time, sometimes years, and the hospital can always appeal to a higher court, dragging the case on even longer.

"Or we go for arbitration," Lenny said. "*If* we lose at the step three hearing."

"That's right," said Rambler. "Arbitration is the faster track, and usually there's no appeal, though the hospital can usually find a loophole if they want to be hard ass about it."

"Lawyers," said Moose.

"Exactly. I would support arbitration."

Regis asked what were their chances of winning the step three hearing. Rambling explained it was an administrative appeal before three hospital VPs. They would reject the union's argument hands down. After that, the union applies for an arbitration judge to hear the case.

"That's too slow," said Regis. "Margie and Woody want to take their leave today."

Rambler admitted, it was a slow process. But the two complainants could take their leave without pay, that was in the contract, they would have to wait for the judge's ruling to receive their pay. With interest.

Allison said, "Everybody I cover is one big bill away from bankruptcy, hoping they don't hit some unexpected bill, like a car breaking down or a trip to the ER." She didn't like that the two workers would be home without pay. Who was going to pay for diapers? Or the PECO bill? "We need to get them to change up like, today," she said.

Woody cleared his throat. New to the sewing room discussions, he said. "Of course, the financial burden will be difficult for us. But it's more important that we win this thing for all the employees who come after us. I can pinch my pennies until the case goes to court if I have to, but most folks don't have that financial cushion."

"You can do a whole lot more," Lenny said. He explained that the grievance and even the arbitration were won before the union sat down with the bosses. He told Woody it would be enormously helpful if he reached out to his friends in the LGBT community to come out to support their fight. Woody promised to start making phone calls as soon as he was back to his desk.

"Better make the calls from home, or at least from outside the hospital on your lunch break," Lenny advised. "You can be written up for using company time for personal calls."

He looked around the room. "How much support for Margie and Woody can we pull from the rank and file? What's the sense in the house?"

Regis said the workers he talked to were pissed as hell that the hospital still discriminated against people because of who they loved. He was confident they would get a lot of support if the union went public.

Allison agreed. "Straight or gay, it doesn't matter to the people I cover, they know a mother's love is sacred. Same for a dad. I think we should call on our friends in the LGBT community to join us on a picket line. Let's raise some holy hell. Let's show Philadelphia what kind of Cro-Magnon creeps are running the hospital."

"I wholeheartedly agree," said Woody. "I mean, they're already suing poor patients who get behind paying their bill. When is it gonna end?"

Lenny looked at Moose, who smiled a deep satisfied smile. The wily steward knew that Moose had a long memory. He recalled how they'd both been arrested years ago for taking a militant stand in a labor dispute against the hospital. It had been a pain in the ass, but they'd won the day. Moose was signaling he'd do it all over again just to spit in the boss's eye.

"Okay, we go for arbitration if we lose the third step grievance. But before we get that far we organize informational picketing outside the hospital. We invite the media, the politicians, church leaders and the LGBT organizations. We shame the bastards, maybe they'll give in and we won't have to go to the judge."

"What day is the Step Three?" asked Allison, opening her cell phone calendar app.

"Wednesday, twelve pm. I got that time to coincide with the protest, we can get all our people to take their lunch the same time."

"That's a busy time in the kitchen," said Moose. "We'll get out there at two, keep the heat on the bosses."

Regis, Woody and Allison left to begin spreading the word and Lenny said he would notify Margie about their decision. It was going to be a busy week, and that wasn't taking into consideration his investigation of Nasir's murder.

When it rains it pours, Lenny thought. Only in his work as a hospital custodian, it usually rained down feces and urine.

<>

Back on the ward, Little Mary had just finished wiping down a discharge bed, a stack of fresh linen waiting on the bedside table. Lenny came in to help make the bed. They stretched the fitted sheet over the mattress. The fabric was old and worn, they had to be careful not to tug too hard for fear it would rip.

"Man, these bosses are so cheap, they can't even buy new sheets for the patients," said Mary. "I got a neighbor, says the hospital took her to court for a bill of a hundred-fifty dollars. She can't afford a lawyer and they took it out of her monthly pension. That ain't right!"

Lenny said, "The VIP patients get maids and jacuzzi's in the room, the poor get sent from the ER to another facility after they've been 'stabilized for transport.' It's all a part of the Croesus plan to admit a lot more upscale patients."

"I hear they get Hollywood types coming in under fake names for, like, plastic surgery and stuff."

"I heard it, too. Anything's possible in this circus."

Lenny told his friend they were going to hold an informational picket on Wednesday outside the hospital protesting the hospital's refusal to grant paid parental leave to the LGBT workers. Mary promised to bring the issue to her church, their pastor was a strong believer in equal rights for gays and trans. She believed she could bring half their parishioners to the demonstration. "Hell's bells, half 'o them are retired, they got time on their hands and they're itching to raise some holy hell. You think Jesus wouldn't be out in the street with us? He sure would."

Although Lenny had no religious beliefs, he had a deep respect for the social justice advocacy that some of the

Philly churches supported. Having attended so many funerals for workers who died too young, he'd heard many a sermon condemning the unequal treatment of manual laborers and white-collar management. The union forces were beginning to gather: it was war, and they were ready to march.

26

Detective Joe Williams tossed the forensic report on his desk and scowled. No surprise, there had been no usable fingerprints from the exit door where Clair Bowen and her accomplice had apparently exited the hospital. The alarm box in the hallway was equally uninformative, there was no way to know how long it had been disabled or by whom. From what Lenny had told him, it could have been out of commission for weeks or months.

Examination of Nasir's body had been equally fruitless. They had found no stray fibers or hair, no skin cells beneath his fingernails, and no sign of the weapon used to deliver the fatal blow. They did find that he had engaged in sexual relations not long before his death, but could not determine who his partner had been. They also found a small quantity of cocaine in his jacket pocket. It was thought to be recreational, there was no sign Nasir had been trafficking in drugs, but they would have to scrutinize his bank records, he may have had a deposit box where he kept cash made from drug sales that he didn't want discovered.

A search of the Nasir residence so far had yielded little of value. There were no records of Clair Bowen/Nasir purchasing an airline ticket, car rental or suspicious bank withdrawals: nothing to suggest she had planned to walk away from the marriage and her life in Philadelphia. There had been no activity on her credit or debit card since her disappearance, and calls to her cell phone went to voice mail.

Although Williams considered the wife a suspect in Nasir's death, he had to keep open the possibility that she had been killed as well. Perhaps by her husband, who had been on duty the night she disappeared.

Williams realized he needed to talk to the night staff, which would mean some serious overtime: if he didn't find them at home, he'd have to interview them at work, which would be after eleven PM or at five in the morning. And since Nasir had been a royal bastard, there was bound to be a long line of workers who hated his guts.

Nasir. When the night nurse Catherine reported Clair Bowen missing, why the hell didn't he tell anyone that he was married to the patient who disappeared? That was suspicious as hell. On top it all off, he couldn't interview the suspect because the bastard was dead.

And then there was Lenny Moss. Williams was pleased Lenny had shown him the trick door. And the canny custodian had been accurate in his assessment of the patient's room, something definitely didn't add up there. The detective wanted to get a look at Clair Bowen's medical records, but that would require a court order, which took time.

It was time to interview the workers on the night shift, more than a few had a grudge against Nasir. He decided to shake the tree, hard, and see what fell out.

<>

Where do you get blood to fake a GI bleed?

That was the question Lenny was pondering all afternoon as he emptied the trash liners one more time and cleaned up a soiled bathroom. He had no idea how someone might fake such a disease, but he had a pretty good idea who to ask. He made his way to the blood bank, where a busy technician was signing out two units of blood for a patient in the OR. The tech releasing and the nurse receiving the blood had to each check the medical record number, patient name and patient date of birth, and they both said aloud the blood type: "O Positive."

Once the tech was free, Lenny asked if he could answer a hypothetical. Stu was a compactly build fellow with a goatee and long hair tied in a bun. Lenny knew the man played in a band, but he couldn't recall what sort of music he played.

"Hey, Stu, how's the music business? You playing any more dive bars this Fall?

The tech chuckled. "Yeah, that joint in Manayunk was pretty skuzzy. I was surprised they didn't have sawdust on the floor."

"Spittoons in the corner."

"No shit." The tech waited patiently for Lenny to get down to business.

"I've been trying to figure something out," said Lenny.

'Okay...'

"You heard about the woman who disappeared from Seven South last week, middle of the night." Stewart admitted he'd heard something about it. "She was supposed to have a GI bleed, but I have a nagging sense she was faking it. How could somebody do that?"

Stuart stroked his straggly beard and thought a moment. "Well, it's easy enough to swallow fresh blood. Human or animal, wouldn't make much difference."

"Yeah, Doctor Stone in the ER told me they wouldn't have a reaction to it the way you would from a bad transfusion."

"That's right. Think of the steak you order 'rare.' You want it red and juicy, right? The meat is full of blood, but your body doesn't reject it. It absorbs the nutrients and you crap out what you can't use for fuel."

"Where would she get this blood? I mean, you have to account for every unit you get, right? People sign for it and all."

"Two people have to sign for every unit that's released from the lab...for a transfusion. But outdated blood goes to the medical waste. It ends up incinerated."

"Huh. Someone could pick it out of the trash?"

"That would be risky, you never know what's in the sealed barrels. But you could pick up a unit if you had a friend in the blood bank, or in housekeeping. I know workers who take blood home to feed their rose bushes. It's against the rules, but you know how it is."

'I do indeed. They must have killer flowers."

121

Now it was Lenny's turn to ponder the problem. After a moment he said, "Okay, so how could I prove this was not a real GI bleed? That the patient swallowed somebody else's blood."

"You got any sample of the blood she threw up?"

"N-o, I don't have it. I bagged all her personal belongings and turned them over to the nurse. Her sweater was stained with blood, pretty heavy. Could you use that?"

"Sure. I could check the blood type, see if it's not a match to her own. If she was ever typed, that is."

"You'll have the records, she used to work in the NICU, she's a nurse: Clair Bowen-Nasir."

"Great, we'll have her blood type then. Get me a sample, I'll get you an answer. And if the blood *is* the same type, I can do a DNA test to see if they're from the same donor, that'll be definitive."

As he turned back to work, Stuart added, "Hey, give me some lead time on the LGBT demo, will you? I want to bring my son, he's in college at La Salle."

"Sure. You want to bring him because..."

"'Cause he's gay, and I want to give those bastards a piece of my ever lovin' mind."

27

Returning to the ward, Lenny found Mimi in the medication room and whispered in her ear did she know what became of Clair Bowen's belongings? Mimi held Lenny's hand palm up and wrote with her fingertip, C-O-P-S. He was disappointed but not daunted. It meant another call to Detective Williams. He decided to wait until the end of the shift and use what he'd learned in the blood bank to barter for more information about the missing woman.

Lenny leaned in close to the nurse and whispered he needed to ask her one more thing. Mimi took the GPS unit from around her neck, opened one of the drawers in the medication cart and gently placed it there. She closed the drawer slowly, making no sound.

"Shoot," she said in a whisper.

Lenny explained that when he had interviewed Catherine Thursday evening, he felt she might have been holding something back. He couldn't say what exactly, but there was something nagging him about the talk.

"Funny you should say that, Lenny, I had the same feeling when I gave her report the night Clair Bowen disappeared. The patient asked me if she could keep the curtains closed around the bed. I figured she was just shy, so I said she could, and when I told Cath, she kind of bit my head off."

"Like she didn't want to discuss it?" Lenny asked.

"Exactly. I thought maybe she and Louis had been arguing, he's been out of work a lot, and with the baby and all..."

"A logical conclusion given you didn't know your patient was going to go up in smoke."

"And a night supervisor was going to get whacked a couple of days later."

Lenny thanked Mimi and tiptoed out of the medication room, bringing a smile to the nurse as she carefully retrieved the GPS unit and placed it back around her neck.

<>

Regis wasn't surprised when Dr. Fingers instructed him to bring Nasir's body to the autopsy suite and set it up for a post mortem, the city Medical Examiner had given them permission to conduct the autopsy. Once the young assistant had all the instruments set out and the body laid out on the stainless steel table with the gutters for draining blood and other fluids, a troop of young physicians, medical students and a physician's assistant came into the room. Fingers instructed them all to don TB masks, informing them that Nasir had tested positive for TB on his annual physical exam, although he had a negative chest X-ray and no signs and symptoms of active disease.

"Anyone like to tell us how an individual can have a negative chest x-ray and a positive PPD test?"

The young physicians were hesitant to answer, not wanting to look dumb in front of the chief pathologist. Finally, a student raised her hand. "The person could have had a sub-clinical infection. That wouldn't show on a routine X-ray, you would need an MRI for that."

"Very good," said Fingers. "It's important to also always consider bovine TB. It's rare in the States, but we sometimes see immigrants who consumed unpasteurized milk or cheese that harbors active TB. The GI tract is the portal of entry, hence, a normal chest film."

As the pathologist began to make a circular cut of the top of the skull to expose the brain, Regis took up the water hose to flush any blood or fluid off the table. He asked if the physician had been able to determine the time of death. Fingers said the body had been fully chilled when it was discovered, so he could only say the body had been in the locker a minimum of six hours, though it might have been twenty or even more.

Dissection of the skull confirmed that a massive cerebral hemorrhage was the cause of death. Opening the chest and abdomen, Fingers found evidence of chronic liver disease, obstructive lung disease — the man had smoked cigarettes and cigars — arthritis in the hip and knee joints, and fungal infections in three toes.

In other words, no surprises, and nothing to tell them who had ended the life of Mr. Boris Nasir. But before sewing up the body, Fingers made an interesting finding in the man's genitals. He pointed to the small scar on the underside of the scrotum.

"It looks as if our philandering husband didn't want to risk getting hit with any paternity suits," he said.

Regis agreed, that would be just like Nasir to have a vasectomy. No need for condoms, no feeling for the women he abused.

<>

Near the end of his shift, Lenny went down to the basement, cursing Moose under his breath for always nagging him to spurn the elevator and always take the stairs. His first stop was the Housekeeping Department, where he filed a grievance over Margie's suspension with the office secretary. Then he made his way to the IT department. He found Ali's desk clean and bare.

"Didn't Ali come into work today?" he asked the young woman in the cubby hole opposite. The woman told him no, Ali was out sick. That worried Lenny. The last time they spoke his friend had complained about experiencing bad headaches. He hoped the young man's condition wasn't serious. Having worked in the hospital for many years, Lenny knew there were a host of diseases that can attack the brain: a blood clot or a bleed into the brain, a tumor, even an inflammation of the sheath around the gray matter, and all of them were bad news.

He made a note to try calling Ali one more time. Hopefully the condition would turn out to be just a migraine, nothing more, his friend sure deserved to catch a break for a change.

28

At home before dinner, Lenny sat in his favorite chair while Patience got the children in their Halloween costumes. Malcolm and Takia wanted to try them on and see how they looked the day before the big day. Takia was dressed as a Princess of Egypt, complete with scarab and tiara, a sort of a wand for anointing visitors, and a veil she could lift off her face. Malcolm had his vampire cape, black shirt and pants and black sneaks and fake teeth with the long canines. The only thing missing was the fake blood running down his face, he was willing to hold off on the final touch for now.

Patience sent them downstairs after the kids conducted a full review in front of the mirror. Malcolm rushed up behind Lenny and bit him on the neck, hard.

"Ow! Hey, what's going on?!" he cried. The boy laughed and told Lenny he was now a demon servant who had to obey his every command.

"And what are you commanding me, oh mighty vampire master?"

"You will let me eat all the candy I want for breakfast until it's all gone."

Lenny said he'd do what he could, but his mom had the final word on what they ate. The best he could offer was a candy dessert on the way to school, a compromise Malcolm quickly accepted.

As the children went back upstairs to change into their pajamas, Lenny's cell phone chirped: the ring tone told him it was Regis Devoe.

"Hey, Re'ege, what's up?"

Regis told Lenny the results of the autopsy: cerebral hemorrhage, as expected. He added that Dr. Fingers could not determine the time of death, only that the body had been in the cold locker at least six hours, it would take that at least much time to reach the temperature of the room.

"So the bastard could've been there for ten hours, maybe longer," said Lenny.

"That's about it. Do you know when anyone saw him last?"

"No, but I'll try to find out, thanks. See you tomorrow. We've got a lot still to do for the demonstration on Wednesday."

"Yeah, we got to energize the troops. We're gonna kick some serious ass."

Lenny had just closed his phone and was looking forward to a double shot of Evan Williams when the annoying instrument rang again. He looked at the identifying name on the screen and cursed softly: Margie Aquinos.

"Lenny! It's Margie! Lenny, you gotta help me, these cops wanna take me downtown and lock me in a room! They say I haven't been 'forthcoming.' What the fuck do they mean forthcoming? I told them everything I know, which is a whole lotta nothin'!"

"The police are going to question everybody who worked with Nasir on the graveyard shift. Don't let them scare you, it's just part of the drill."

"Yeah, but I ain't never gonna get my job back if'n they arrest me for murder!"

"Try to stay cool, Margie. Don't let them get you upset, you might say something they can twist around and use against you. Why do they say you haven't told them all that you know?"

"Hells bells, they don't believe I spent the night in my car in the parking lot. And they keep goin' on about my saying I was gonna put a hurt on him. You know that's just talk!"

"I know that Margie, but the police have to suspect somebody, and your threats give them a reason to suspect you. Have you got a lawyer?"

"Sheila already called and got me somebody, he's gonna meet me down the station."

"Good. Say nothing until you speak to your lawyer. Remember the golden rule: Nobody talks, everyone walks. Can you remember that?"

"Yeah, I got it. Thanks, Lenny. Pray for me!"

"Okay, Margie, just stay cool and keep quiet until your lawyer arrives. The police already have a prime suspect, I don't think they're going to keep you for long."

Lenny hung up, not telling the beleaguered housekeeper that he had a hunch the police were going to focus on Clair Bowen as their prime suspect, a battered woman who couldn't take it anymore would be an obvious target of their investigation.

He hoped it wasn't Clair. Or Margie. Or anyone on the night shift. But if it wasn't a worker with a grudge or the wife, then who the hell battered Ralph Nasir's head in and left him in the cold storage locker?

29

After the troubling phone conversation with Margie, Lenny mixed himself a double shot of Evan Williams and settled into his chair to think about the issues he was facing. Priority one was the step three grievance and the upcoming demonstration to pressure the bosses. The union staff at the office had made calls to several human rights and LGBT organizations. Everyone had responded with promises to take part in the demonstration, which would kick off at noon on Tuesday, while workers who punched out at 3 PM would swell the event, as would friends from the churches and synagogues. There would be TV coverage that would broadcast on the 5 pm news as well.

The union had also sent word to the entire Philadelphia City Council, all the progressive church groups, and student activist groups at all the local colleges and universities. Plenty of opportunity for speeches and railing against the hospital's anti-gay policy.

Moose was using his graphic arts skills to design the flyer, which would be given out at the hospital entrance as the day shift came on duty. The noon time rally would probably be the largest crowd of the day, while more workers would join the protest as they finished their shifts in the afternoon.

Lenny didn't expect any arrests, but he'd notified Dave Rambling, just in case. Everyone would have the union phone number written on their arm in case they were arrested, be they workers or supporters. If there were a lot of arrests, calls would be made to volunteer lawyers and the greater human rights organizations that had legal resources behind them.

And on top of all that, there was Catherine's pending termination. She had no union, the RNs had given up the drive to join his service workers union, but the all-RN Pennsylvania union UNP apparently still hadn't collected enough signed pledge cards to call for a vote. So, Catherine's only support was a labor lawyer she could hire...or Lenny.

He went over the interviews he'd conducted: Louisa, the nurse's aide who had been working with Catherine on that night. She had been awfully tight-lipped, which was a surprise. Lenny had helped her with immigration issues for her mom, he thought they had a trusting relationship, but Louisa had said as little as possible. Was she afraid of being disciplined the same way that Catherine was?

Then there was his visit with Catherine. He felt the nurse had not been altogether truthful, a not uncommon occurrence in his business. Knowing he had to get hold of Clair's bloody clothes, he decided to call Detective Williams and explained the situation.

He checked his watch: just past ten, not *too* late to call Williams. When the detective answered the phone, his first words were to ask wasn't it past Lenny's bedtime? Lenny ignored the crack and explained why he called: the blood bank had the ability to test the blood type of the blood that Clair had vomited up. Lenny wanted to determine if the vomited blood was not Clair's, but the police had taken custody of the clothes. Could he bring the evidence in to the hospital in the morning to be tested?

Williams said, "We have a forensics lab that isn't entirely useless you know."

"Yeah, I'm not knocking your crime lab. It's just, if the sample *is* the same blood type, it still could be from somebody else. The hospital lab can compare the fricking DNA of her actual blood with the blood on the clothing."

"And that's going to help me solve the Nasir murder case how?" asked Williams.

"I don't know exactly, but if the blood isn't a match, at least it would confirm that she faked her illness. If you figure out why she did that, I have a hunch it will shed some light on Nasir's murder."

"Keep your hunches to yourself, I don't need to hear them." Williams was silent on the phone for a moment. Finally, he said, "You're a royal pain in the ass, you know that, Moss?"

"So that's a yes, I take it."

"I'll see what I can do, no promises."

Before hanging up, Williams told Lenny he had bad news. The District Attorney was looking at the housekeeper on the night shift, Margie Aquinos, for the murder of Boris Nasir. The "lesbian mom," as he put it. "She hated Nasir and she threatened to do him bodily harm. We have a witness, and we have it on tape, and she claims she spent the night in her car, *in* the hospital parking lot."

"You gotta be kidding me. You want to build a murder case around an offhand remark she might have made? They can't find Clair Bowen to press charges so they're sticking it to one of the workers? And you're going along with them?"

'No, I'm not *going along*. I told my captain I thought the wife Clair Bowen should be suspect number one until we find her, or we find her body. He's hemming and hawing, could go either way."

"Can you keep your captain from arresting Margie a little longer? Give me a little more time to tease out what happened that night in the hospital. Can you do that?"

"You have some new information I don't know about?" said Williams.

"It's nothing you don't already know. She was an abused child and abused wife."

"Yes, I got that from the Employee Health doctor. Clair Bowen does have a motive for offing her husband, plus, she used to work at the hospital, she could have known about the exit that wasn't alarmed. She could have slipped back inside the night Nasir was killed without being seen, clean as a whistle."

"I never understood that phrase. How exactly is a whistle clean?" said Lenny.

"You want us to issue an arrest warrant for Clair Bowen instead of Margie Aquinos?"

Lenny had no answer for the detective. He didn't even have an answer for himself. But he did have a plan: Catherine had not been particularly helpful when he interviewed them. He decided to give her one more chance to tell what she knew. Not that he could compel an answer. He had a good idea just what leverage he could use to get the nurse to open up.

"Give me a day to poke around. I really think I'll have some information you can use to crack the case."

Williams made no promises, leaving Lenny on his own.

<>

Finally settling into bed, Lenny took up a copy of the newspaper, but his mind wouldn't focus. Patience asked if he was going to offer to coach Malcolm's soccer team. When Lenny admitted he knew nothing about the game, she told him in this age group it was more about getting out on the field and having a good time, not winning. "Besides," she said, "in a lot of soccer games they don't score a single point, it's decided in the shoot-out at the end."

"Shoot-out? It sounds like a wild west show."

"It's wild, I'll give you that," said Patience. She asked him if he remembered when they were first talking about getting married how worried he was the children wouldn't bond with him because he was white.

"Anxious? I was scared shitless. I was more scared of them then I was of you turning me down."

She kissed him on the cheek. "Did you really think I would turn you down? A sweet, hard-working man like you?"

Lenny asked Patience what got her to agree. She told him it was because everyone knew he was the sort of man who always came home from work to his family. He didn't fool around, he didn't gamble or drink — well, no more than any man did — and he was so good with the kids.

"I remember the first time you came over. You read to the kids their bedtime stories."

"They were a lot younger and easier to impress back then."

"Well you impressed the hell out of me that night. You enjoyed the children's stories as much as they did! I saw right from the get-go you're just a big overgrown kid, and that's the kind of man I want my children to grow up with."

She settled her head on his chest. "I don't mind having a man with muscles, either."

"And calloused hands."

"Gentle hands, Lenny. And a generous heart."

30

Arriving at work well before the start of his shift, Lenny went to the Communications Office, where the dispatchers sat in their cubicles listening to complaints and requests from patients and passing them on to the relevant nurses on the wards through their GPS units. He knew who covered the upper floors, which included Seven South.

"Jason, you got a sec for me?"

"Oh, hi, Lenny." The young dispatcher was not happy to see Lenny. He knew it would probably mean a union issue that involved the dispatch service, and he hated to be in the middle between management and worker.

"I understand night before last you reported a worker making threatening noises about Boris Nasir. Is that right?"

Jason hemmed and hawed, but eventually admitted he did make a comment to his supervisor. "It wasn't a report exactly. It's just, they tell us all the time, we have to keep our ears open for any threats of violence. It's an employee safety issue. You know, for the women workers, and it wasn't the first time I heard her talk trash about her supervisor."

Lenny agreed, it was extremely important to maintain a safe working environment, especially for women workers who could face sexual harassment or worse. He asked what exactly did the worker say. Jason said she had promised to "put a hurt on Nasir," something along those lines.

"And you know who it was, how?"

Jason said he recognized Margie's voice.

"Did you specifically hear the nurse wearing the GPS unit address Margie Aquinos by name?"

Jason admitted, Catherine never used Margie's name. He claimed he was pretty sure it was Margie, because Margie "had a mouth on her," and the woman he overheard was quite strong in her words.

Lenny pointed out that the little microphone on a GPS unit was a low-frequency device that had piss-poor sound quality. Was Jason willing to swear under oath in a deposition before a bunch of lawyers that he was absolutely sure he had heard Margie Aquinos's voice?

Jason got scared at the promise of a deposition before lawyers. He agreed, he couldn't be sure, it was just an assumption.

Lenny thanked him for his honesty and hurried on, he had more people to talk to, and the morning was already underway.

<>

Hurrying to the Housekeeping Department, Lenny strode past the secretary and straight into the office of Director Childress. He reported his conversation with the dispatcher, pointing out that the nurses had already filed an invasion of privacy civil suit against the hospital for not being allowed to turn the device off during their tour, not even when they were in the bathroom.

Childress scowled. As much as took satisfaction in disciplining workers in his department, he knew that a statement made to a supervisor did not always carry over to reliable testimony in a deposition. But Childress had an ace up his sleeve, and he was eager to play it.

"We take threats of physical violence seriously in this facility, Moss. What that employee said amounts to a terrorist threat. You above all should know that. Safety is our number one priority."

Lenny didn't bother pointing out that forcing housekeepers and nurses to work short handed day after day posed serious risks to the patients as well as to the staff. He would save that argument for another day and another forum. For now, he stuck to the point that Jason was an unreliable witness, and that under oath he would be unable to make a clear identification of the individual in question. The audio quality from the GPS units was piss poor, it could have been anybody. The hospital had a losing case, did Childress really want to fight over it?

The cunning shop steward added one more piece to his argument: what was the point of pursuing a threat against a man who had been murdered? He wasn't in any danger.

"I take your point," said Childress, placing his elbows on the desk and lacing his fingers together. "But I have an audio recording of the conversation. It won't be difficult to confirm whose voice it is." Before Lenny could object, the supervisor added, "We're talking about a threat of violence, I can't overlook it, that would set a dangerous precedence. An employee can't threaten the life of another employee, end of story."

Lenny left without trying any more argument. He got it. Childress wasn't going to stick his neck out by showing compassion for a worker. It would have to go to the next level. But the case was not necessarily a losing one: Lenny thought he might find a way to get the hospital to back down on Margie's termination, although it would be like betting all his chips on an inside straight.

<>

Arriving on Seven South by the elevator, Moose's physical fitness harangues be damned, Lenny found the Seven South aide Louisa emptying a bed pan sloshing with urine in the patient's bathroom. Asking the aide to step out into the hall, he warned her that Margie had been interrogated at length by the police and was a prime suspect in Nasir's murder.

"Ain't no way Margie had anything to do with that mess!" said Louisa. "No way no how was Margie part of it."

"But she was heard threatening the supervisor. That looks bad for her. The cops are going to charge her any day now. Maybe today. If you know something that can help her…"

"I'm sorry I told that police detective what Margie said! I didn't want to, but he said he had it all on tape, I was talking with Catherine."

"The dispatcher heard it on her GPS unit."

"Yeah, probably so. If you start lying to the cops, they figure it out and then you're in a heap of trouble yourself." Louisa fought back tears, she felt such terrible guilt at having implicated her friend and co-worker.

"Just tell me everything you know about that night. If it puts Margie in the clear, it's all good."

Louisa pouted her lips and took a deep breath. When she let it out in a long sigh, she said, "If you wanna know something about what happened to the woman that up and disappeared, ask Catherine. She was in charge that night. She can tell you a whole lot more than me."

"What can she tell me?"

Louisa shook her head sadly. "I don't know all the in's and out's. All I know is, us girls got to stick together. That's what Catherine told me that night, and that's what we did."

31

Moose carried the box of pastries under his arm as he walked past the Seven North nursing station. The two nurse's aides from the night shift were busy emptying the last foley bags, measuring the volume of urine and reporting it to the RN, who would enter it in the patient's computer database.

"Hey, Cocoa," Moose called to one aide, "I brought some sweets for you and Carmen. You want I should put them in the kitchen?"

"Don't do that, Moose, somebody's likely to come by and dig through it. Take it to the lounge, we'll meet you there in a jiff."

He made his way to the lounge and waited. It wasn't long before the two aides came in, their work done, it was time to grab coats and purses and get on home to be sure the children were going to school and not sleeping in all morning.

"Oh, boy," said Carmen, "chocolate cream filled eclairs, my favorite!" She grabbed up two, wrapped them in paper towels and stuck them in her over-sized purse. "What's the occasion?"

"Me and Lenny are helping out the Seven South folks, they're in a heap of trouble for that patient went missing last week."

Cocoa said, "Yeah, we heard about that. It's a sorrowful shame to blame the workers just 'cause a patient decided James Madison wasn't for her."

Agreeing, Moose asked if they had been on duty the Wednesday night of the incident. Both women said they were. He wondered if they had seen the patient on their ward. They had not. He asked if anybody had come through their ward who maybe didn't belong. Like, a man in a surgical scrub suit, hat and mask pushing a cart? He might have gone through the passage over to Seven South.

Cocoa said she didn't remember seeing anybody like that, it had been a busy night, a confused patient had to be restrained and an old lady had fallen going to the bathroom when she was supposed to be using the bedpan and not get out of bed.

Carmen said maybe she saw somebody like that, she was pretty sure. She had been assigned to the far end of the ward, way away from the passageway Moose was talking about. But she thought she did see somebody like that early in the shift come past her with a cart. She didn't know the guy and he didn't speak to her.

"Was he delivering supplies to your ward? Laundry, maybe, or restocking the isolation carts."

"No, I didn't see him refill anything. Besides, Margie takes care of the linen closet and restocking the isolation carts."

"Could he have been from pharmacy?"

"Nah, we know the one pharmacy tech on nights, and it wasn't him. Pharmacy wears navy blue shirt and pants, they don't wear no surgical gown."

"I sure hope the patient's all right," said Cocoa. "Usually when a woman runs off in the middle of the night, she's either running to love or running from hate."

Before leaving, Moose asked the two women if they were going to come for the demonstration in front of the hospital on Wednesday. They told him mad horses couldn't keep them from calling out the bosses who treated the workers like servants and like they were the high and mighty kings.

32

As Lenny began his shift, he had the feeling that an avalanche was rolling down a mountain toward him that was going to bury him six feet under. The Step Three grievance hearing was scheduled for the next day, and it wasn't clear if the union would bring out a thousand people at the noon time rally or a dozen.

The LGBT organizations in the Delaware Valley promised to send people, so Lenny was confident they would have those activists as a core cadre. Other hospitals were sending union members, since the HSWU had contracts in twelve hospitals and nursing homes in the Philly area.

He'd sent out a raft of text messages, a mass email and another post on the union social media page. There had been few responses so far, but the posts had gone out before the start of his shift, so that was no surprise, he would check online at morning break.

On top of the labor issue, he had to deal with the Nasir murder investigation and Clair Bowen's disappearance. And then there was the likelihood that the police would arrest Margie Aquinos for the murder, even though the evidence was as thin as the strand of a spider web.

Little Mary saw the somber look on her partner's face and tried to cheer him up. 'Yo, Lenny, you gotta lighten up. Why so glum, we're gonna kick the boss's ass tomorrow!" She reminded him that union members had "illegally" posted flyers calling for the picket line in all of the staff lounges and bathrooms, despite threats to fire any worker caught with the flyers on hospital property. As fast as the supervisors tore them down, they were posted right back up again, driving the bosses crazy.

The flyer had an image of a baby carried by a stork with the word GIVE ME LEAVE, DON'T MAKE ME GRIEVE as the header. It wasn't the most militant headline the union had posted, but one of the younger stewards had come up with it and Lenny didn't want to discourage the fellow's literary efforts. When a rank and file member steps up to the plate, you have to cheer him on.

"Yeah, I know I haven't exactly been my cheerful self lately," said Lenny. "Normally I'd be excited about joining a picket line, it's just all the other crap I have to deal with."

"All the more reason to share the load. Isn't that what you've been preaching to the rank and file for years?"

Lenny had to smile, Mary was spot on. He knew he had a habit of taking on too many union responsibilities for himself instead of struggling with members to carry a greater part of the work. That's what had moved Regis to become a steward, the young man channeled his anger into organizing, and he was doing great with it. He knew that Regis, Moose, Allison and others had been talking up the demonstration. Countless workers had posted the union flyers in bathrooms, elevators and staff lounges.

In short order he and Mary had all the trash from the ward collected. Lenny was mopping the hallway while Little Mary cleaned a discharge room left over from nights, a patient had died and the body not taken away until the shift change.

Seeing Moose coming through with the breakfast cart, Lenny joined him. As the dietary aide carried a pair of breakfast trays into a patient room, he told Lenny that one of the aides on Seven North midnight shift was pretty sure she'd seen the mystery man in the surgical scrub suit with the cart the night Nasir was offed.

Lenny asked Moose if anyone had seen Clair that night, but Moose admitted no one had seen her on the sister unit. One thing they were sure of, the guy in the surgical outfit, whoever he was, wasn't delivering anything to their unit. Housekeeping stocked the linen, and pharmacy had their own messenger to bring STAT meds.

Moose promised to give out more flyers about the up-coming protest and went on giving out the breakfast.

Stepping into the Housekeeping supply closet, Lenny sent Ali a text message asking if he was feeling okay and if he'd seen that doctor about his headaches. Lenny had a sinking feeling that his friend had suffered some major insult to his brain. The man lived alone, he could be lying on the floor of his living room in a coma. Or dead.

Not sure what to do next about his friend, Lenny decided to drop in to the IT department and see if they had any news about him. If Ali had not been in contact with his department, maybe he'd seen a doctor at James Madison, it was a logical place to find a physician. He decided to ask Dr. Primeaux to check the hospital database, see if his friend had any recent blood work or x-rays.

He shuddered at the thought of his friend ending up on Dr. Fingers' autopsy table.

33

All morning long his phone chirped with messages about the upcoming demonstration scheduled for noon the following day. Joe Hagarty with Philly Labor Talk radio promised to cover the event, as had several of the reporters for the local union newsletters. He hadn't heard from the major TV news stations, but those announcements had been left to the union staff, so Lenny had to just have faith they had all been contacted and would attend. He wanted a good spot on the evening news.

When break time came, he hurried to the sewing room to meet with the core union leaders and make any last minute decisions.

<>

Without enough battered old folding chairs to accommodate everyone, Birdie spread out towels on the floor so the younger members could sit. She counted fourteen people by the time Lenny and Moose came in: a good show of union solidarity.

"Okay, listen up," Moose said. "We got the retirees coming at eleven-thirty. We got PROUD coming at twelve. Our working members who are off today will be there, and those on their lunch break will join up, too."

"You got enough signs?" a young member asked. Regis assured her the union had printed dozens of signs demanding paid leave for LGBT workers, equal treatment for all, and Patients Over Profits, too.

"The Mayor comin' down?" asked another member. Lenny said he'd been told the Mayor had a prior commitment that he couldn't get out of, but several groups had been pressuring him to attend, so maybe he'd show up. Several city council members promised to come.

"Any chance to make a speech," an older member stated.

Lenny reminded them that the members tasked with security would be wearing red T-shirts and red arm bands. They would keep the protesters on the sidewalk and off the street and grounds, leaving the police no legal basis for arresting anyone.

"You think they'll cave at the grievance hearing?" Moose asked, alluding to the negative public relations the hospital management was bound to suffer for refusing the paid parental leave. "The money it would cost them is peanuts. They spend more on hair products and dry cleaning."

That got a laugh, but Lenny wasn't smiling. "Let's see how large a crowd we draw. If it's big — I mean rock the casbah big — then yeah, we have a good shot of winning and avoiding the long wait for an arbitration judge. But don't get your hopes up too high, Reichart and his gang are all about taking, they won't give anything up unless the pain we give them is greater than the loss."

<>

Catherine had heard from Mimi about the demonstration scheduled for the next day. She was sorely tempted to attend, if just to give Mother Burgess and the rest of the pack of jackals a piece of her mind. But she had baby Lilly to care for, and she didn't think standing on the picket line would help get her job back.

Louis agreed, as did the labor lawyer they'd hired, Mary Donkers, a perky, optimistic RN who earned her law degree and gone into private practice. Now she defended hospital workers against wrongful terminations and helped patients who had been injured in the hospital file civil suits. Donkers reassured Catherine that Mother Burgess had no factual basis for threatening the nurse's license. As an "at-will" employee, the hospital did have the right to terminate her without showing cause.

But the scrappy young lawyer thought they could still turn that around by arguing in court that management was wrong to put the blame for a patient eloping on a nurse, when the GPS unit showed that she had made her hourly rounds on schedule. The computer records show the aide had taken the patient's vital signs at the required start of the shift, and all medications had been dispensed property up until the moment the elopement was discovered.

Still not optimistic about returning to James Madison to work, Catherine went down to the basement to start the laundry.

<>

With all the calls, text messages and workers coming up to him on the ward, Lenny's morning flew by like a downhill racer. He wanted to call Detective Williams to see what news the man had for him, but his steward duties kept him occupied every minute of the day. Not to mention all the housekeeping work that had to be done, there was no way he could leave his job to talk to the detective.

Support for the LGBT workers was higher than he'd ever seen it. It was more than the blanket unfairness of the policy: workers were tired of being pushed around. The issue gave them a place to focus their anger, which had been pent up for too long.

You win the war before you go into battle. He rolled that familiar piece of wisdom over in his mind once more. It was all in the preparation: in rallying the troops, recruiting support from the community, enlisting the progressive politicians and the liberal media pundits. At the union office they'd been making calls and sending out mass emails. Wednesday would tell if they had enough to make the administration back down.

Lenny made his way by the stairs (cursing that damn Moose!) to the IT department, hoping to find Ali at his station. He went to his friend's desk, but the chair was empty. Again. A young woman with dreads and a lovely Jamaican accent who in the next cubicle told Lenny that Ali hadn't been in touch since he called out sick Monday morning. "Did you speak to him?" Lenny asked. The young woman told him, no, Ali had left a voice message.

Lenny went over to his friend's desk to see if there were any indication of how bad the situation was. The desk was bare, the binders on a shelf neatly aligned and standing perfectly straight.

Lenny's locker in the housekeeping locker room and the housekeeping closet he shared with Mary on Seven South were forever a books, union papers, lotion for his hands and extra clothing, he could never keep the areas tidy. If it weren't for Patience, their home would be in the same state of disarray.

Lenny tried calling his friend one more time, but the call again went to voice mail.

"Christ, don't let him be dead," Lenny mumbled, now deeply worried about Ali. He hurried back to Seven South, climbing the stairs and arriving at the landing out of breath. As he entered the ward, he saw a very large security guard standing in front of the housekeeping closet. The door was open and another guard was ransacking the room, turning over buckets, pulling bottles of cleaning solution and wax off the shelf.

"What the hell is going on?" Lenny said, approaching the guard in the hallway.

"Searching the closet. We got a report there was illegal materials being stored there."

"*Illegal?* What are you talking about? We stock cleaning supplies, we don't have anything dangerous. This is a load of BS. I'm calling the union, we don't—"

Lenny stopped in mid-sentence when he saw the second guard standing in the doorway holding a raft of papers.

They were the flyer the union had been clandestinely posting about the upcoming demonstration for LGBT rights.

Possession of the flyers on hospital grounds was immediate grounds for termination.

Lenny asked to see one of the flyers. The guard handed a page to him. Lenny held it up to the light and studied the flyer. He ran his thumb and forefinger over the paper, feeling the texture. Satisfied, he handed it back to the guard, who told him he was to report to the housekeeping office asap.

As soon as the guards left the ward, Lenny called Regis and filled him in on the new threat. When Regis asked how Lenny was going to handle it, the wily steward said he had a plan, but he needed Sandy, the old security guard who was a good friend to the union, to do him a favor. Hearing Lenny's plan, Regis promised to take care of everything and would meet him in the pathology department as soon as he had everything set up for the disciplinary charges.

Ready for battle, Lenny went to tell Mary he would be off the ward one more time today, but this time he couldn't be written up for abandoning his post.

34

While Housekeeping Director Norman Childress couldn't suppress his glee at finally getting grounds for firing Lenny Moss, Joe West kept his unsmiling poker face as he stood in the Housekeeping office overseeing the action. The Director of Hospital Security was known for never smiling. And never missing a chance to enforce a discipline.

"We found fifty-five copies of your union flyer in the Seven South housekeeping locker, Moss. It is a disgusting piece of garbage that attacks this administration with inflammatory, scurrilous charges of sexual discrimination. You know the rules. You know what you're in for. Unless you want to try and pin the blame on your partner." Childress tapped the stack of flyers with his finger. "But that wouldn't be in keeping with your noble posture, friend of the working man, now would it?"

Lenny kept his own poker face, having dealt with Childress and countless other supervisors over his long career as shop steward, not to mention amateur detective. "I guess I'll just have to walk the plank all by myself. Looks like I'll finally have the time to paint the kids' bedrooms, my wife's been nagging me about it for ages."

Getting no response to his smart aleck remarks, Lenny reached into his shoulder bag and pulled out his own copy of the illicit flyer. Placing the paper on Childress's desk, he arched a single dark eyebrow, foreshadowing a gambit that wiped the smile of the director's face.

"*This* is a copy of the union leaflet that union members have been handing out on the *public sidewalk* outside the hospital, on their off days, not violating a single hospital policy or city ordinance."

Childress picked up the flyer, glanced at it and said, "What's your point, Moss?" The supervisor handed it to Joe West, who gave the paper a more thorough investigation.

"If you feel the weight and texture of the flyer that the *union* produced, you will note it is a twenty-four pound stock, *rag* paper with a brightness rating of ninety-five. The flyers that your guards "discovered" in the Seven South housekeeping locker are printed on a cheap twenty-pound paper. It looks like it has a brightness of, maybe eighty at best."

"So?" Childress put the union-produced flyer on his desk. "What's your point?"

"My point is, the flyers you are using to accuse me were not produced by the union. They were copied in the hospital."

"Oh, yeah? How do you figure that?" Childress was chewing his lip, not so confident as when Lenny first entered the office.

Lenny pulled out another flyer. He held it up for Childress and West to see. "This is a copy of the union flyer that was made on the copy machine in *your* security office less than an hour ago. You can see the weight and texture are identical to your 'discovered flyers.'"

"Yes, but —"

"And what's even *more* interesting is, the color of the typeface in the union flyer is not black, it is deep navy blue, while the color in the security office-copied is straight black." Lenny explained that the security office machine had only a black cartridge, it had no color cartridges. The union copy machine had a six-color set of cartridges. When the union machine produced a flyer with a simple black typeface, it used a mixture of colors to produce the dark characters, but those characters were never actually black, they were always a midnight blue. The flyer Lenny had introduced clearly had a different colored typeface than the flyers from the housekeeping locker and the security office.

Childress took another look at the union flyer. He didn't bother asking how Lenny was able to use the Security Department's own copy machine to produce the evidence, that investigation would have to wait. For now, the director had to choose whether to apply the termination or not. He chewed his lip and glanced over at West, who stood ramrod straight and said nothing.

"Okay, Moss, here's what I'm gonna do. I'm going to issue you a written warning about harboring illegal materials in your work closet. But if I find even one more flyer in your work area, it's good-bye and good riddance."

Childress told Lenny he could pick up his written warning at the end of his shift. Lenny got up and returned to his ward, relieved and just a bit cheerful at having gotten the best of his boss.

35

Lenny had just hung up his mop for the night and was closing the door to the housekeeping closet when he saw Detective Williams coming toward him with a bag under his arm.

"You weren't going to leave work without checking out that far-fetched theory of yours, were you, Moss?"

With a long, deep sigh, Lenny agreed to stay. He called Patience and asked her to take the car, he'd get home later, then he led the detective to the blood bank, where the day shift was about to go off duty.

"Hey, Stu, sorry to bother you at the end of your shift," Lenny said.

The blood bank tech glanced at Williams, saw the bundle in the detective's hand. "That the missing woman's clothing?"

Williams said it was and handed it to the tech. "How long will it take you to test it?"

"Give me five, you can wait out in the hall." Stu wasn't fond of the police, having been beaten and arrested protesting the mayor over the bombing and murder of the Move commune several years before.

Out in the hall, Williams asked Lenny what was his latest thinking on the case. Lenny asked him which one, Clair's disappearance or Nasir's murder. When Williams suggested they were one in the same, Lenny admitted he had been thinking along the same line.

"I have been following a promising line of inquiry, if you'll forgive my cop-talk" Lenny said. "I'll tell you everything, but I need some information from you, first."

"You need it because..."

"Because you have access to information I can't get, and I need them to fill in the blanks. What have you found out about Clair Bowen?"

The detective told him so far they had found no evidence that Clair had made plans to flee the jurisdiction. She hadn't bought airline tickets, at least not with a credit or debit card. She had made no recent cash withdrawals, had sent no emails to an accomplice. Her passport was still at home, so she hadn't left the country, at least, not legally.

"No use of her credit card for any purchases, I guess," Lenny added.

"Nothing. Her car is still parked in the street in front of her house. Far as we can tell, all her clothing and luggage are still at home. And just to be sure we didn't miss anything, we took a cadaver dog over the property, but she didn't indicate any body buried in the garden. Clair Bowen more or less disappeared without a trace."

Lenny asked if there was any sign in the video surveillance of Clair returning to the hospital the night that Nasir was killed. Williams admitted there was none, but pointed out she could have returned by way of the silenced emergency exit. He indicated it was time for Lenny to tell everything he knew.

"Like I told you on the phone, I don't think Clair really had a GI bleed. I think she was faking it. The blood bank throws away donor blood that's passed it's expiration. If you had a friend in the blood bank..."

"Something a nurse who used to work in the Neonatal ICU could easily have..."

"That's right. It wouldn't be difficult to get someone to give you a unit. Some people take blood home to feed their roses."

"Must be prize winners," said Williams.

"No doubt. The point is, she could swallow the blood before coming to the ER. And if she swallowed activated charcoal —that's a medication they give for drug overdoses — it would make your stools black."

"Like a GI bleed."

"Exactly. Now, one of the nursing staff working nights on Seven North thinks she saw a guy with a limp go through to Seven South that night. He was wearing surgical scrubs and a cap and mask, so she couldn't see his face, but she did see he was pushing a cart that was covered with a sheet.

"Which could have held the extra pillows used to make the bed look occupied and clean clothes for the woman to wear," Williams said.

"That's what I'm thinking. He wore that mask to partially conceal his face, and he kept his face turned away from the one surveillance camera, so he must have known where they were."

"A hospital employee."

Lenny arched a single black eyebrow. "You know who on the staff walks with a limp? I should say, *walked* with a limp."

"No, who?"

"Boris Nasir."

Williams chewed on the tidbit of information for a moment. "I'm not buying it. How could Nasir take the pillows down so he can kill his wife and remove the body when he didn't know she was even in the hospital? Remember, she was admitted under her maiden name."

"A name that he knew all too well," Lenny said.

Williams didn't think Nasir made a habit of looking over the names of every patient admitted to the hospital, he would be too busy chasing skirts. Lenny agreed, a supervisor only heard about special admits, like a VIP or an emergency open heart case that required calling in a whole team, not a routine admission from the ER.

Clair keeping the curtains closed: Lenny thought it was likely out of fear of being seen. Of a danger to herself. Since she never left her room, the nurse's aide on nights confirmed that Nasir would not have seen her in the bed when he made his rounds.

The tech came out to the hall with a folded slip of paper. He handed it to Lenny, then set off for the exit to take his leave. Lenny unfolded the paper. It reported: Clair Bowen blood type, A Positive. Specimen blood submitted, B Positive. No match.

Williams took the slip from Lenny and tucked it in his pocket. He grumbled that now his case was even more complicated than before. Why would Clair fake a GI bleed? Did she leave voluntarily or was she abducted? Did Nasir know of his wife's admission or was it a coincidence he was killed a few days after she disappearance?

Williams asked if Lenny had any idea who might have helped her get away, assuming she did elope and was not abducted. Although Lenny had his suspicions, Louisa had told him "girls had to stick together," he decided not to share that piece of information just yet. Instead, he said he was still in the dark. But he had a good feeling about the case. "Give me another day to sniff around, and no jokes about my nose, it's the only one I've got."

Williams told Lenny to keep in better touch, then he walked off the ward, leaving the weary custodian longing for a long rest and a disabled cell phone.

<>

When he finally made it home, Lenny was in state of mixed emotion: happy he'd beaten back his supervisor's effort to fire him — for now — anxious that the coming demonstration would not be the big, raucous affair that would pressure the bosses into changing their paid parental leave policy, and just plain exhausted from the constant weaving and dodging he had to do to push the union forward.

Patience could see that her husband was dead tired. She suggested he settle into his favorite easy chair and read the paper or listen to some nice jazz and offered to pour him a strong drink. Lenny didn't argue, even though he wanted to make a dozen phone calls to the stewards and community organizers he'd been in contact with. He decided to make the calls after dinner. Besides, the plans were set, the allies in the social justice organizations promising to come out in support, as well as the local liberal politicians.

He settled into his chair, kicked off his black work shoes and opened the Daily News to the sports section. The Eagles were not doing well, a big fall from their Super Bowl victory of the past. Not that Lenny was a huge sports fan. But he tried to keep up with the major teams, including some of the international soccer teams so he could hold up a conversation with the workers from a dozen different countries.

Before he got through the first article, he was fast asleep. Patience quietly placed a coaster over his drink to keep it fresh and told the children to keep the noise down until dinner.

36

Patience was about to wake Lenny for dinner when she heard a loud *knock, knock, knock* on the front door. The sound awakened her husband, who turned his head to see who Patience was bringing into the house.

It was Margie. She looked even more distraught than usual.

"Lenny! What am I gonna do if they haul my sorry ass off to jail? How's my baby gonna grow up with a single mother to raise her? This shit's driving me ever loving bonkers!"

Getting out of his chair, Lenny asked Margie if she wanted a drink. Margie asked if it wasn't too much trouble, maybe a cup of tea? With a lot of sugar?

Patience promised to put the kettle on, saying, "We were just about to sit down for dinner, you're welcome to join us."

"No, thanks, I appreciate it, but I've gotta get back home, Sissy is worried sick about me. I just need to ask your husband something."

While Patience saw to the tea and checked the dinner warming in the oven, Margie settled on the edge of the sofa. Her foot was vibrating and she cast her eyes all around the room.

"So what do you want to ask me?" Lenny studied his friend's face, looking for signs of what was really going on. Having interviewed countless workers who were in trouble on the job, he had learned that the first story he heard was not always the complete one. Nor was it altogether truthful. He'd learned to listen to the voice as much as the words, and to study the eyes for signs of subterfuge.

"It's like this. You remember I told you how I spent the night in my car the time that bastard Nasir was killed."

"Yeah..."

"I didn't exactly spend the *whole* night *inside* the car, sleeping."

"I didn't think you did. You've got to get hungry some time. And you've got to pee at least once a night, that's only human."

Margie's face showed some relief at Lenny's understanding.

"Did you go to the WaWa on Germantown Ave to get something to eat?"

Patience quietly placed a cup of tea on the table beside Margie. The anxious woman thanked her and took a sip. "Nah. I don't like their food. Except for the soft pretzels, those are pretty good. And they have spicy mustard."

Trying to keep the conversation focused, Lenny asked Margie where did she go to eat and to use the bathroom.

"In the hospital, where do you think?"

Lenny asked if she went in by the Emergency Department. Margie told him she wasn't that stupid, she used the emergency exit that had the alarm disabled. Lenny wondered how many workers knew of that little secret.

"O-kay. Where in the hospital did you go?"

"The vending machines, of course, I had some coffee and a sandwich. And then I... I went to the department for the rest of my things."

Neither surprised nor irritated, Lenny accepted that the woman who was suspended with the intention of termination had gone to the very department where the discipline had been meted out.

"I needed to get my stuff from, you know, the shared locker. See what I mean?"

Lenny understood Margie, they had a shared locker in the men's housekeeping locker room as well. It was "assigned" to a fictitious worker. Anyone who needed to keep something on hand that could get them in trouble if it was discovered in their own locker used it. Lenny kept a stack of the union leaflets there as well.

"So you got your stuff and then you went back to the car. Is that right?"

"Yeah, pretty much."

Lenny gave her a quizzical look. Margie admitted she'd taken the stairs up to Seven South, just to have a talk with Louisa. Nobody saw her there and she kept away from the security camera, she was sure of that.

When Margie asked how much shit was she in, Lenny told her it was pretty deep, but she shouldn't lose hope. The police hadn't arrested her. Yet. She had to trust her lawyer, Donkers knew her way around the court room, and the hospital. He promised to call the lawyer and offer to help any way he could, and he advised her to stay away from the hospital until the termination issue was settled.

Margie promised to not go back inside the hospital, but she swore she wasn't going to miss the demonstration, she was bringing her daughter and her wife to it, it was an important day. A big day.

"My baby's gonna learn early you got to stand up for your rights," she said. At the door, Margie confessed she was scared of going home, she was afraid the police might be waiting for her.

"Ask Sissy to go outside and look for an unmarked police car with two plainclothes officers in it, they were usually pretty easy to spot. Margie brightened at the suggestion and promised to call as soon as she was in the car. She thanked Patience for the tea, even though she'd only drunk a little bit of it, then she wrapped her arms around Lenny and almost lifted his feet off the floor in a bear hug.

"You the best, Lenny, you know that? The bestest of the best."

Closing the door behind her, Lenny went to get fresh ice for another drink, then he called the children down for dinner. He was worried that Williams had seen video images of Margie in the hospital the night Nasir had been killed, the hospital parking lot had good camera coverage, they would show her leaving her car and walking toward the facility. Plus, it wasn't all that easy to dodge every camera in the place. It was looking more and more like Margie's arrest was imminent. Maybe tonight.

Lenny was not surprised that Williams had kept quiet about Margie's suspicious movements the night that Nasir was killed. Apparently, Lenny wasn't the only one in the relationship who kept some of his thoughts to himself.

37

Wednesday morning brought fresh union flyers taped to bulletin boards in the staff lounges, posted in the staff bathrooms, in the ward kitchens and the supply closets. There was an electric thrill in the air. Workers coming through Seven South delivering meds or supplies or linen gave Lenny a thumbs up or a fist bump. They were fired up and eager to go out on their lunch break to protest.

Even the nurses were excited, though they couldn't express their support out loud due to the hated GPS units. Instead, they used crudely coded words to express their support. Mimi told him with a wink, "I heard there were thunder storms in the forecast today at noon. Thunder and lightning." Lenny said he had brought his foul weather gear, the weather was no problem.

Regis met Lenny on Seven South at 12 PM. Together they rode the elevator down to the first floor, stopping on every floor in between to pick up stewards and rank and file supporters. By the time they reached the ground the elevator was as packed as the ER on a Saturday night.

They spilled out onto the lobby, then hurried on to the main entrance. Standing at the head of the broad marble steps, Lenny looked out on a huge crowd of people, many holding up home-made signs protesting the hospital's policy and demanding that President Reichart be fired. There were union retirees with their grandchildren, having taken them out of school for the occasion. The grinning kids held their grandparents' hands and swayed with the rhythmic chants rising from the crowd.

There was a giant multi-colored banner with the slogan: PARENT PRIDE. The LGBT community and their supporters had come out in big numbers, doubling the size of the protest had it been union advocates alone.

A group of men from the Philadelphia Gay Men's Cho-
rus performed a Gregoreian chant that echoed through the
crowd, while a line of drag queens danced along the sidewalk holding a giant banner declaring DRAG QUEENS
FOR JUSTICE! The photographers and videographers for
a dozen news organizations had a field day, and Lenny was
grateful for the extra news coverage that the LGBT per-
formers would bring the union.

Woody and his husband had their young son Julian at
the demonstration. The boy, just turning one year old,
rode on Woody's shoulders. One of the Queens scooped
up the little one. "Oooh, what a sweet baby, can I take him
home with me? I'll teach him to sing like Caruso. Or even
better, Judy Garland!"

Woody told her that Alex wanted their son to be a gym-
nast, but he wanted him to be a dancer. "Well, you can't
tell kids anything, they have a mind of their own," said the
dancer, giving the lad a kiss on the cheek.

Police cars with their lights flashing were parked on the
opposite side of Germantown Ave, the officers watching
and signaling to street traffic to keep moving. A truck driver slowed and leaned heavy on his horn, raising a shout of
approval from the protesters. A local TV news truck was
parked half up on the sidewalk, its antenna pointed to a
satellite somewhere in the sky as a reporter stood in front
of a cameraman giving an update on the scene.

Rambler, the union lawyer, stood beside a minister who
invoked the words of Dr. Martin Luther King, Jr. in his
prayer for the hospital workers who had been grievously
mistreated. Then a member of the Philadelphia City Council took up the microphone. The Councilman talked about
the city's "remarkable human rainbow" and the "city's
heritage of combating racism and sexism and all forms of
discrimination and oppression. As he spoke, his assistant
gave out postcards with the Councilman's smiling face on
the front and a list of his legislative accomplishments on

the back, with a web site where voters could make a donation toward his next campaign.

When the councilman's speech was over, Rambler led the huge crowd in a chant: "NO JUSTICE, NO PEACE! ... NO JUSTICE, NO PEACE!" The mass of chanting protesters filled the sidewalk and spilled onto the hospital grounds.

The union lawyer reminded the crowd of why they were there: to give equal rights to the LGBT workers at James Madison Hospital; rights that included equal pay and equal paid leave. Then Rambler asked Woody to say a few words.

Lenny had told Woody that he would be asked to speak, but the man was overwhelmed by the size of the crowd. Dressed in a powder blue suit, dark blue fedora, button-down shirt and scarlet bow tie, he took up the microphone and pulled out a paper with his notes. He looked at the paper, then looked out at the thousand-plus supporters spilling over the sidewalks, all smiling and looking at him expectantly.

Stuffing the note in his pocket, Woody said, "My dear, dear brothers and sisters, in our wonderful union, in our LGBT community, in all of Philadelphia: this is a great honor to be asked to speak to you. You probably know by now that the hospital in their infinite wisdom has rejected my request and another gay worker's request to be paid while we take our leave to bond with our children. I thank you from the bottom of my heart for your support. Your support means more to me — to us — than I can put into words.

"But I want to speak about another issue that you may *not* have heard about. I work in the billing department. That doesn't make me the most popular employee in James Madison. I don't get the love the nurses and the doctors do. But all of us in the department do whatever we can to help our clients find an affordable way to pay any outstanding bills.

"Well, lately the hospital has taken the poorest of our clients to court to collect on those bills. Poor people, struggling to pay their rent and to buy their medicine. The hospital in some cases is attaching their pay, or even their pension or welfare check, do you believe, to collect the debt. People are forced to give up their rent money or their food money or their medication money. And why? Why is the hospital taking this action? They do it to discourage poor people from seeking admission to the almighty James Madison Hospital and to attract a more wealthy, a more profitable clientele."

Boos filled the air and many protesters shook their signs in anger.

"I hope that after we win this battle for LGBT rights, we take up this administration's cruel medical gentrification policy, and make our hospital a place of refuge for the poor and the lost, the homeless and the out of work, as the Lord and as we want it to be. Thank you."

A huge cheer went up from the crowd. As Woody stepped back into his place among his PRIDE friends with tears in his eyes, they hugged him and shook his hand.

Lenny followed Regis and the others down the steps to the demonstration. When the chant died away, Rambler handed the microphone to Lenny. Lenny looked over the crowd for a moment. "Brothers and sisters, we are saying NO to discrimination against our gay and lesbian co-workers! We are saying NO to policies that target the poor and the retirees living on pensions! We are saying no to insulting and degrading supervisors! And we are saying YES to solidarity with all of the workers who sweat and sacrifice in this cursed health factory!"

The crowd raised a thunderous cheer. People blew whistles, rang bells, clapped hands and shook their signs above their heads.

"In a little while our union lawyer and a couple of delegates are going in to a grievance hearing about this criminal policy with three administrators..." Boos and curses rang out at the mention of the bosses. "They will give us the usual BS about hospital costs and 'fiduciary responsibility,' as if stealing wages and benefits was some kind of natural law. But all the time their lips are moving, they're going to be listening for *you*. For you who stand with our LGBT workers and demand a fair treatment for them. And it's *your* voice, not mine, that will determine what they rule in that meeting. Stay strong, brothers and sisters. With your help, we will win this fight."

The crowd cheered as Lenny turned and walked back to the entrance with Dave Rambling. Their cheers grew into another chant: "NO JUSTICE, NO PEACE! NO JUSTICE, NO PEACE!"

38

Lenny squared his shoulders like a boxer going into the ring as he passed back through the hospital entrance with Dave Rambling, the union lawyer. "You ready for this?" he asked the lawyer.

"I'm locked and loaded, brother."

They walked down the administrative wing, their feet making no sound on the plush carpeting. Rambling reached out with a fist and knocked once on the heavy oak door.

"Enter," a deep voice inside replied.

The two union officers stepped into the administration conference room. Lenny saw the familiar long, dark stained wooden table and the three plush armchairs positioned on one side of the table with three plush, well-fed administrators settled into them like pampered cats.

Two simple cloth-covered chairs on the opposite side were waiting for them. Rambling dropped his battered leather bag on the table while Lenny dropped his backpack on the floor. They pulled their chairs back and settled in.

"Did you get it all out of your system out in the street, Mister Moss, or are you going to yell slogans at us today as well?" Arthur Ivory, VP for Patient Services, placed his hands on the desk, his diamond-studded cuff links shining in the light.

"Let's just review the grievance, shall we?" he replied. Lenny made the case that denying paid parental leave to a parent just because the union contract did not specifically require it overlooked the principle of equal treatment. "You are discriminating against these workers because of their sexual orientation," he added. "That violates the spirit of the contract in and of itself."

"If it isn't in the contract, it doesn't exist." Dixon Hill, the Chief Financial Officer, was a plump gentleman who looked like he would be right at home managing a large bank with thick marble walls. Whenever Lenny crossed swords with the man, he imagined the smug bastard would be smoking a thick cigar if it wasn't for the hospital-wide smoking ban.

Rambling had opened a file and looked over his notes. He pointed out that gay and lesbian workers were a protected status under Pennsylvania and Federal statutes. The case law was consistent, judges ruled consistently in favor of plaintiffs who sued for discrimination based on sexual orientation.

"If we take this to court, you lose, you pay *us* for the court fees, and the papers plaster your homophobic pictures all over the front page."

"The courts are changing," said Donaldson, VP for Strategic Planning, which Lenny knew was a code name for attracting upscale patients and denying services to the working class and poor. "They are moving back to a more sensible position on gay rights. You could lose in court. Then, who would look stupid in the press?"

"Lose in *Pennsylvania?*" Rambling had on his best look of astonishment. "In your dreams! Public sentiment is overwhelmingly in favor of gay rights, the courts are not going back on past rulings, not in *my* lifetime."

Rambling added that the protest outside would be all over the evening news. The papers would carry the story on their web site by nightfall, and in the morning it would be front page headlines. "Do you really want to see another, bigger demonstration next week? And the week after that?"

"We have a fiduciary responsibility to our shareholders, we can't be paying people who are not working," said Hill, the CFO. "Where will it end? Should we pay people to stay home and care for an elderly parent? A sick pet dog?"

"Your bottom line seems to be doing just fine offering paid leave for biological parents. Adding the LGBT parents isn't going to break the bank, you can count the number of cases you would face in a year on one hand."

"We may decide to eliminate paid parental leave altogether," said Donaldson. "Costs are constantly rising, Medicare is cutting its reimbursement rates, insurance companies are withholding reimbursement for ninety days, sometimes a hundred-twenty. We have to look at—"

"No justice, no peace! No justice, no peace!"

The sound of voices echoed down the thickly carpeted hallway and penetrated the heavy oak door. The chant grew louder as the protesters grew near. Donaldson looked at Hill, who glared at Lenny.

"If you think you can decide this hearing with more of your street theatrics, you have another thing coming!" said Hill.

"You wouldn't believe me if I told you I had nothing to do with the protesters coming into the facility, but I didn't. That was not in our plans, although it's not something I have a problem with."

Rambling stood up, went to the door and opened it. Moose, Regis, Allison and Margie burst into the room, followed by LGBT protesters decked out in bright, multi-colored clothing. Even their hair was streaked with decorative colors.

"L-G-B-T, equal rights for you and me!"

A security guard tried to move the demonstrators out of the room, but the protesters locked arms and stood along the wall, chanting and staring down the three administrators.

Hill stood up and walked around the table to Lenny. "Listen, Moss, we are not about to hold a hearing with this rabble in the room. You have to clear the room."

Lenny asked if the administrators would seriously consider the union position if the protesters left. Promised they would give the union a fair hearing, Lenny huddled with Moose, Regis, Allison and two of the LGBT activists. He suggested they take the demonstration out into the hall and sit down there. They should leave room for people to walk through, they would be arrested if they violated the fire code regulations and blocked the passageway, but otherwise they could form a chain and line the entire hallway all the way out to the main lobby.

There were some heated back-and-forth comments. Margie was adamant about staying in the room, she wanted to grab one of the bosses and rip his balls off for denying her the right to bond with her child. Allison tried to calm her, saying they should stay out in the hall and let their union representatives speak for everyone.

Finally, the protesters agreed to leave. Even Margie left, but she promised to be right outside the door, ready to come back if needed.

Once the room was cleared, Lenny told them, "Look, this issue isn't gonna go away. We're going to hold protests every week until you make paid parental leave universal for all parents, period. People are gonna think twice before coming to James Madison for their care. They'll go someplace else. You want to 'grow your business?' It's not gonna grow as long as the press is broadcasting your policy on the six o'clock news."

The three administrators leaned in together and whispered among themselves. There were frowns and scowls, head shaking and fists dropped hard on the desk.

As the bosses argued, Lenny and Rambling sat back, sensing the momentum was shifting in their direction. They could see it in the faces of the administrators, who no longer had the arrogant appearance they had projected at the start of the hearing.

Lenny told Arthur Ivory that he needed a sidebar conversation. Stepping to a corner of the room, Lenny told the Patient Services Director that he wanted Margie Aquinos's discipline reversed as part of the grievance decision. When Ivory tried to claim he knew nothing about the disciplinary case, Lenny cut him off in mid-sentence.

"She's one of the two workers denied leave. What would you say to a co-worker if you were denied time with your newborn child?" Lenny kept to himself the thought that the administrator probably sent his children away to boarding school and spent little time with them as infants.

"Threats of violence cannot be tolerated, Mister Moss. You know that as well as I."

"She was just blowing off steam. She has a perfect attendance record. Never been written up, always willing to work overtime when asked."

"That won't convince anyone to let her back on the job."

Lenny looked back at Rambler, then returned his gaze to Ivory. "Listen, Childress told me in clear language that he had recorded Miss Aquinos's voice. He's been using the nurse's GPS units to *record* workers' speech. How would the hospital like it if I called a press conference and announced that kind of brazen violation of privacy?"

"The courts have ruled employers have the right—"

"I don't give shit about the courts, it's a hideous invasion of privacy. If the nurses learn West has been recording their voices, they'll be signing union pledge cards in droves."

Seeing Ivory's face softening, Lenny offered to enroll the worker in an anger management program and not return her to work until she had completed the course and been signed off by the therapist. He didn't bother to add that more than one manager had been afforded the same conditions when they had been accused of threatening bodily harm to a worker.

"I'll put it to the others," said Ivory. "I can't make any promises."

Lenny went back to his seat and told Rambler of the conversation. The lawyer asked if Lenny had promised not to tell the nurses about the hospital recording them. Lenny grinned. Such a promise never crossed his lips.

After a long wait and a lot of muttered complaints, Hill, the CFO made a proposal: "We will grant paid parental leave for these two cases and these two alone," he said, "but only if the union goes on record that the decision is not a precedent for future applications for leave."

177

Lenny looked at Rambling, who leaned in and asked if there were any other LGBT couples about to have or adopt a child. Lenny didn't think so, though he couldn't be sure. Rambling suggested to Lenny that they would win the paid leave rights in the next contract, even without citing a past practice, and if another case like Margie's or Woody's came up before then, they could threaten more protests if another LGBT worker was denied the benefit.

"Okay, we can live with that," Lenny told the administrator. "And Margie Aquinos?"

Hill agreed to the terms Lenny had proposed, adding, "We will draw up the papers, you can sign them at the end of your shift."

Lenny accepted the cheap shot. He could have picked up the agreement any time during his shift, but Hill wanted to stick it to him by making him wait until he punched out.

Lenny and Rambling stepped out into the hall. The multi-color outfits gave the drab hallway a cheerful, festive air. The protesters stood up when they saw the union representatives.

"We got the paid leave," Lenny said.

A cheer rose up, shaking the walls. Margie hugged Lenny, then she hugged Dave, then she hugged several of the protesters.

Everyone started down the hallway making for the main entrance. Standing at the head of the broad marble steps, Rambling announced the union victory. A cheer went up from the crowd. As television crews crowded around the lawyer, asking questions, delighted, laughing workers slowly made their way back into the facility. A festive mood swept over the workers. Sharing the elation, Lenny went back to his ward, taking the steps two at a time, he had so much adrenalin pumping through his body.

Stepping out on the ward, his good humor came down a notch as he realized he still had the damned murder-disappearing patient investigation to deal with. He hoped Margie's reinstatement wouldn't be interrupted by an arraignment in front of a judge.

39

After punching out in the Housekeeping office, Lenny went to the Administrative wing to pick up a copy of the agreement. As promised, the CFO had left two copies, one for him to sign and retain, the other to sign and leave with the office secretary.

Lenny signed both copies with a bold flourish, which brought a contemptuous look from the secretary. "Who do you think you are Mister Moss, John Hancock?"

"No, I'm just an old union man with a mop and bucket."

He deposited the agreement in his backpack and hurried out to meet Patience at the main entrance. Stepping out into the sunlight, he was surprised to see his wife on the sidewalk in front of the hospital speaking with Margie.

"Margie! I thought you'd have gone home and get some sleep. Aren't you working tonight?"

"Sleep? How d'you expect a body to sleep after what we got done today? I'm high as a kite, and there ain't no drugs involved!"

"I'm happy for you, Margie. But you're coming to work tonight, aren't you?"

"Sure I'm coming to work, I've got three more shifts to pull, and then it's good-bye, James Madison, I'm off for six whole blessed weeks. I'm gonna read to my little girl and sing to her and give her hugs and kisses until she passes out from so much love!"

"Good for you, Margie. I'm so glad. I guess you haven't heard any more from the police."

Margie's joy vanished in a heartbeat. True, the police had not been waiting for her when she got home the night before, and they hadn't come around the house today, either.

"Maybe I convinced them when they interviewed me down the station. I told 'em if I'd done killed the bastard, he'd be cut up into pieces and thrown out with the medical waste. My lawyer says they have to have some real evidence before they charge me with murder, and they ain't got squat."

"Margie, we have got to get you into steward training, you're what this union needs, I swear to god!"

She kissed him on the cheek. "Soon's I get back from leave, my brother. Soon's I get back from my leave....with *pay*!"

<>

At home that evening, Lenny offered to help make dinner. Patience kissed him on the cheek and told him she had dinner covered.

"What was that for?" he asked.

"For being such a good man, and for winning such a big victory for the union."

He reminded her they had won bigger battles in the past. Like when the new owners refused to honor the contract because it had been signed by the previous administrators. That had been a knock down, hard fought battle, but they had won in the end. And then the hospital threatened to withdraw from the health and welfare fund, which would have bankrupted the fund and left the retirees with no pension, no health insurance. Another bitter battle, another big union victory.

Lenny pointed out they still had to get new language in the contract for full LGBT rights when they went into bargaining next year. Patience couldn't see how the hospital could deny them the rights, but Lenny wasn't as confident they would get the new language in writing.

Patience agreed, they were bastards when it came to negotiating a union contract, they always began by threatening to take benefits away. But it was still a huge win, because the bosses were thinking about taking paid leave from *all* the parents, straight or gay. This stopped them in their tracks.

"And," she added, thumping him on his chest, "every victory builds solidarity in the rank and file. You've been telling me that for years, Lenny. *Years!*"

"God help me, I've created a trade union monster." Lenny kissed his wife and went into the kitchen to help make dinner, warning his wife he had a gigantic appetite, there better be meat and potatoes on his plate.

"You peel the potatoes and put them in water, you'll have potatoes." She handed him an apron and a potato peeler and took a roast out of the fridge to season just the way he liked it.

40

Lenny parked the car across the street from Catherine's house and sat a moment looking at the house. Having interviewed many a reluctant witness in the course of his union steward duties, he knew it could be challenging to convince a worker to reveal facts that might be embarrassing. Or incriminating.

Catherine was a good-hearted woman. She cared about her patients. She'd been scared to death that her baby might be born with terrible deformities during the Zika virus outbreak the year before. Then she went through a serious depression, Mimi had told Lenny about it and how the lactation nurse had helped the new mom get past it.

The women had stuck together. Helped each other. There was a powerful network of women helping women in the hospital. They called it the "Pink Patrol," where when one woman was being abused or mistreated by a male supervisor, they called a "Code Pink" and woman from several departments came to support the woman aggrieved.

Lenny had a hunch something like that had been the case with Clair Bowen's elopement in the middle of the night. A woman in the blood bank could have supplied the outdated blood, Catherine could even have been the one to pick it up. She would have been helping an abused wife escape her brutal husband.

He made his way to the front door and rang the bell. It sang a lullaby and faded out. A moment later Catherine opened the door.

"Sorry to come without calling first. I was in the neighborhood, so..."

"Louis is just putting Lilly to bed. You can come in, but you have to be extra quiet."

Lenny promised to talk in a whisper and tried to walk softly into the living room. He sat in an upholstered chair, enjoying the soft cushion and the way it let him settle in as if for the night.

"What are you coming by for?" Catherine cast a suspicious eye on Lenny as she perched on the edge of the sofa.

"Well, you know already, Mimi asked me to try and find out how and why Clair Bowen disappeared from Seven South in the middle of the night. She had some perverse notion that I could help you in some way."

Catherine admitted she knew what Mimi had done, her co-worker had called Catherine and explained it all to her.

"Did you find out what happened?"

"Not all of it, no, but a good part of it. Quite a lot, actually."

Catherine's smile faded at Lenny's last words. She slowly lowered herself onto an upright chair, staring at Lenny and seeming to hold her breath.

He told the nurse he strongly suspected Clair did not have a bleeding ulcer at all. That it had all been a very clever ruse. She had obtained a unit of outdated blood from a friend in the blood bank — a woman she would have gotten to know from her years working in the NICU — and swallowed it to make it look like she had a bleeding ulcer.

When Catherine challenged him to name evidence to back up his "wild theory," Lenny went over the incongruous findings that he and Dr. Stone had described: the normal blood count, even after receiving intravenous fluids, the utter cleanliness of the patient room, when GI bleeders always made a mess of the bed and the bathroom, and the alleged use of aspirin for a knee injury when Clair had an aspirin allergy.

"Maybe she was taking ibuprofen," said Catherine. "The ER nurse taking a history could have heard it wrong, they are busy as hell down there twenty-four seven."

Lenny agreed that was certainly possible. But then there was the video surveillance recording of a man in a scrub suit, his face partially hidden by a mask, wheeling a covered cart from Seven North toward the sister unit. A cart that he believed contained the extra pillows to make up the "body" in the bed and a spare set of clothes for Clair. He added that he knew about the emergency exit door with the disabled alarm, which is where she left the building.

Still seeing that Catherine wanted to deny all of his evidence, Lenny added the coup de grace: the blood that Clair had vomited up was a different type than her own.

He studied her face, looking for signs of guilt. Or of lying. Catherine held a pretty good poker face, but her downcast eyes and slumping shoulders suggested she was hiding a great deal.

"What exactly do you want, Lenny?" There was no warmth in Catherine's voice or eyes.

"Actually, you don't have to tell me much of anything. I have a pretty good idea you helped Clair set up the bed to look like a patient was still in it. I think you watched her slip out by the stairwell as she walked down to the emergency exit with the disabled alarm. I think you did this to help an abused woman escape a rotten bastard of a husband. It's just what a caring nurse like yourself would do."

Catherine kept silent and impassive. A minute ticked by. Then another. Lenny thought he would never get an admission of guilt from the nurse. Nor would she give up any information about where Clair had gone. He was damned and determined to get some new information before he left.

"Before I go I should caution you about one thing."

"What is that, exactly?"

"The police are investigating a murder. I think it's unlikely they will accuse you of the crime, you don't have a motive, but you never know."

"But I wasn't even working when Nasir was killed! I was suspended from duty!"

"True, although since you knew about the un-alarmed emergency door, you could have come into the facility unseen."

Before Catherine could object, Lenny added a bluff. "The police are going to charge Clair with the crime, *when* they find her. And they *will* find her eventually. As the wife of an abusive husband, she is the logical choice."

Lenny couldn't really be sure the police would ever find Clair, he couldn't be certain the woman was alive. Nor could he promise they would charge the woman with Nasir's murder. But he used the threat to try and pry more information out of Catherine. Her eyes opened wide at the suggestion that Clair was wanted by the police, such a threat would haunt her forever.

Lenny went on to tell Catherine that even if the police never did find Clair, they could still charge her in absentia, and they could charge Catherine right here and now as an accomplice.

"But Clair didn't kill her rotten husband! I know she didn't!"

"How do you know? How can you be sure?"

Catherine closed her mouth, having realized she'd betrayed a crucial piece of information to Lenny. She sat silent and still, her eyes fixed on a distant object. Lenny had one more card to play. It was his last chance to get the truth out of the troubled nurse.

He told Catherine that if Clair was never found, the hospital bosses would argue the woman was dead and that she, the nurse on duty, was at least partly responsible for the death. That would make Catherine's chances of getting her job back at James Madison all but impossible.

"To put it plainly and simply," said Lenny, "you keeping silent about what happened to Clair will kill your chance of coming back. It might even jeopardize your nursing license."

He could see the pain and conflict in Catherine's face, knowing she was paying a stiff price for her loyalty.

"I can't say anything, Lenny. I just couldn't live with myself if I did."

He told her he understood, he had been in situations like hers many a time as a union steward. Faithfulness to principles came at a cost. Sometimes the price was all but unbearable.

Catherine stood up, went to the front door and opened it. She stood at the door, speaking not a word, grim-faced and tight-lipped. From fear...or anger...or despair, Lenny could not tell.

"If it's consolation to you," he said, standing in the doorway, "your secret is safe with me."

Driving toward home, Lenny went over what he knew: Catherine had admitted Clair with the plan to smuggle her out of the hospital and away to some safe house. A male colleague, perhaps Catherine's husband Louis, had delivered the pillows and clothes for her escape.

Lenny wanted to believe that Clair was alive, and that she did not go back in the hospital to murder her husband. What would be the point of successfully executing a plan to fake an illness, leave pillows in the bed to buy time and slip out and away if she was going to come back and off the husband she was escaping from?

Which left the unpleasant prospect that Nasir had somehow gotten wind of Clair's plan and killed her before she could escape. Was *that* why *he* was murdered? As revenge for murdering his wife?

But there was another possibility. Assuming that Clair did not kill Nasir, that left Margie the obvious suspect. She had motive aplenty, and she was angry enough to do it. But would she risk going to jail and losing the opportunity to raise their daughter just to murder an understandably infuriating supervisor?

Lenny didn't think so, but there weren't any other suspects in his field of vision. That was the problem: find another suspect. Find the real killer.

He hoped.

41

After punching in at the Housekeeping timeclock the day after their big union victory, Lenny was happy to just take care of his housekeeping duties for a change. Not that there wouldn't be new problems to deal with, somebody was always getting in trouble, some boss was always looking to win favor with a vice president by firing a worker and making it stick.

When Moose came by with the breakfast cart, a big grin on his face, Lenny told him to hold onto his good mood, it wouldn't last forever.

"You gotta dump that cynical attitude, man. Life is too short to always look on the dark side of life."

"I'll watch some Ingmar Bergman movies tonight, maybe it'll cheer me up."

A tray in either hand, Moose took the breakfast into a room, set them down and came out to find Lenny still looking unhappy. "What's eating you, Lenny? We won a big victory, you should be doing cartwheels."

"Ah, it's this shit with the patient who disappeared and the fricking Nasir case. Not that I give a damn who killed the bastard. I promised Mimi I would try to help the night nurse who was fired. But I'm worried she was involved with the patient who vanished. The more I dig into it, the more she looks guilty."

"Yeah, that's a tough nut to crack all right. Glad I don't have to put my forehead into a problem that deep, give me a headache." As he went on to deliver the next pair of trays, he reminded Lenny they needed to go jogging one night this week.

"The jogging trail's closed," said Lenny. "Somebody spotted a wolf prowling in the park."

"Don't even try it!" Moose grabbed two more trays and went on with his work.

Running a dry mop along the floor, Lenny picked up the debris left over from the night tour. Clusters of doctors and students drifted by talking about cases and ducking into patient rooms. A phlebotomy tech passed him with a tray of blood specimens.

Blood. That's where the case began. Lenny feared blood would be where it would end up: a bloody corpse, the missing Clair Bowen found in a shallow grave, or floating in the Delaware River. And he would be no closer to figuring out what the hell happened to both victims.

<>

At break time Lenny decided to see if Ali was finally back to work, his friend had not answered any voice messages, text messages or emails. But the man's desk was just as bare and empty as he had left it, with Ali having left yet another phone message that he was still sick.

Lenny called the Employee Health department and asked would Dr. Primeaux check to see if Ali had made any doctor or clinic visits in the last seven days, explaining that his friend had complained of a wicked headache that sounded serious and had been out sick all week.

Lenny added that he was worried his friend might be avoiding getting treatment for some potentially fatal disease, like leukemia. Or a brain tumor. They always seemed to strike the nicest people, and it was always all of a sudden. Ali had never gotten over the loss of his infant daughter, born premature with major congenital defects. His wife's leaving him hadn't helped, either. Lenny had defended the man at the time for a few incidents at work: bursts of anger, failures to complete assigned tasks.

Primeaux looked through the hospital data base, but found no recent doctor visits. The hospital outpatient pharmacy had not dispensed any medications for him as well. The doctor apologized for not being more helpful and promised to keep an eye open for the man.

The employee health doctor had been unbelievably helpful in the past, getting Ali into counseling and testifying on his behalf at a disciplinary hearing. Transferring to the day shift had also helped, a move Lenny had argued for vigorously. In time, Ali got back to his old easy going self, though a melancholy cloud was always hanging over him, threatening to burst into rain and thunder.

Lenny thought he might make a run out to Ali's house after dinner, in case his friend needed something, like some take-out chicken soup, or god forbid, if he was lying on the floor unconscious. Or worse. And if the man was alive but hadn't visited a doctor yet, Lenny was going to ream his ass and demand they go together the next day to see a physician.

He grabbed a coffee and a donut, took them back to Seven South and enjoyed them in the little kitchen, where Mary was packing some leftover food into the fridge. Years ago, when nurse Gary Tuttle had worked on their ward — Gary was working the ICU now — he asked Mary who the food was for that she regularly collected from the patient trays. Mary had told him it was for her dog, but Lenny knew she was helping raise her grandchildren and the budget was mighty tight. The children were back with their mom, a relief for Mary, but she still took food home, there were plenty of hungry children in her North Philly neighborhood.

"How's that boy of yours doing, Malcolm? He all right?" Mary dropped a tea bag in a cup of hot water and added a dollop of milk.

"Yeah, he's fine. He wanted to play junior football but Patience put her foot down, much to his disappointment."

"That's a good mother, looking out for her son."

"Yeah, she is. I signed him up for soccer. The coach wants me to help with the team."

"What d'you know about soccer? You ever play the game?"

"No, but it can't be all that complicated."

"That's a funny thing for you to say, Lenny, you being the one who's always talking about strategy. Thinking two steps ahead. Psyching out the bosses. Every game has its strategy. You better do some serious reading if you're gonna be any use to those boys."

Lenny promised to watch some video programs that explained the game. As far as he was concerned, it was more about getting outside and running around, burning up energy and having fun, but maybe Mary was right: maybe he could teach Malcolm and the boys something about thinking strategically.

Finishing with his break, Lenny resumed his duties. He rolled out his trusty mop and bucket and began mopping the floor. Unfolding the yellow WARNING WET FLOOR, he set it at the head of a stretch of wet floor and stood for a moment to let it dry.

Strategy. Mary was right. Somebody...or some bodies had worked at developing their strategy. Either Clair and a friend had cooked up a scheme to get her admitted to the hospital under her old maiden name and then elope without being seen, or...somebody realized that Clair was admitted and had abducted or killed her and taken her away by the stairwell with the disabled alarm.

How much did she weigh? He asked Mimi's opinion, who estimated around one hundred thirty pounds. Not a big woman. A strong man could carry her down the stairs, or force her to walk it.

But who...and *why?*

Nasir was Lenny's prime suspect for Clair's disappearance. He had been on duty the night Clair disappeared. And he walked with a limp. Lenny tried to picture exactly how the man walked. He closed his eyes and tried to recall the scene of Nasir chewing him out and then walking away. He couldn't say if it was Nasir in the video or if it was somebody else, the memory was too blurry.

But if Nasir had abducted his wife, then who killed *him* and laid him out in the morgue's cold storage locker? Was that an ironic statement, or just making use of a handy dumping place that would give the killer time to get away.

He tried to imagine Margie killing Nasir and hauling him down to the morgue. She was strong enough, smart enough, angry enough...but he didn't buy it. The LGBT policy came from on high, Nasir had just been the messenger. Margie knew that. If she wanted to hurt somebody, President Reichart would be the logical choice.

He collapsed the yellow caution sign and continued mopping, letting his mind wander as the rhythm of the work put him into a kind of daydream. He wanted to never wake up. He wanted to dream forever.

42

As he was driving home after work with Patience in the passenger seat beside him, Lenny repeated to his wife his thoughts about the double mystery. Like him, she believed the two cases were linked, though she couldn't say just how. She agreed that if Clair had been abducted or killed, Nasir had to be the one who did it. But if the woman eloped of her own free will and was alive and well, it was anyone's guess who killed her husband.

"How about a break, we get pizza for dinner?" Lenny said.

"Fine by me, get a spinach and mushroom for me and Takia, you and Malcolm can pig out on your carnivore diet."

Lenny promised to limit his choice to one meat, though he hadn't decided between sausage or peperoni. "I'll get extra tomato on ours," he offered.

Patience rolled her eyes and didn't bother to comment, but she did call ahead to Golden Crust and placed the order. They brought the pizza home and told the children, who wanted to eat right away. But Patience put the pizzas in a low oven and told them they had to at least start their homework before dinner. Malcolm stuck out his lower lip, but he brightened when Lenny whispered he ordered pepperoni, the boy's favorite, and ran up the stairs to his room to start the terrible burden of math problems.

<>

After dinner, dishes washed, leftover pizza wrapped in aluminum foil for a quick reheating in the oven later and tucked away in the fridge, Lenny settled into his favorite chair, picked up the Daily News and tried to catch up on sports. Patience was on the sofa listening to an audio book, the sound of the narrator a faint hum from her headphones.

Try as he might to read an article, Lenny's mind kept wandering back to the puzzle of Clair Bowen and Boris Nasir. Who, why and when? Catherine had all but admitted that she knew of Clair's plan to elope, although that still didn't rule out foul play. Nasir could have found her in the room somehow and killed her, he was certainly capable or such brutality.

He went with the idea that Clair had escaped her husband and was hiding somewhere. That meant she would be with the accomplice with the limp. If Nasir wasn't the mystery man on the surveillance video, who could it be? Maybe, Louis, Catherine's husband. She was suspended at the time of the murder, so she could have cared for their baby while Louis slipped unseen into the hospital.

But would he commit an act like that? It didn't sound plausible.

"Dear?" he said to his wife

"Hmm?"

"Lemme ask you something."

Patience stopped the program and lowered the headphones to around her neck. "Okay, what?"

"I was just thinking, if the man we saw on the surveillance video was not Nasir, who do you think it was?"

"Somebody else with a limp. Or somebody who pretended to have a limp. After all, if Clair Bowen could fake her stomach ulcer, her friend could certainly fake a limp."

"Yeah, I think that's right. It was someone who knew Nasir and knew about his disability. He disguised himself not to avoid being *recognized*, but to make it look like it was *Nasir* going to Clair's room and doing away with her."

Patience said, "You look surprised. But aren't you always telling me people are never exactly what they seem? They have gifts and secrets and histories you'd never suspect, even if you worked with them for years."

"I said that?"

Patience threw the coaster she'd used to set her mug of tea on at him. "You know you did, don't act dumb."

"Okay, I'll stick with merely looking dumb, I'm good at that."

Patience returned the headphones to over her ears and went back to her story and Lenny continued thinking about the case. It was clear that once again, nothing was what it seemed. The GI bleed had been a fake, and so was the limp.

Very clever.

Who had that kind of cunning mind? Not Margie, she was a straight up in-your-face person: direct and without guile. Lenny couldn't see any of the other housekeeping or messenger staff on nights developing this kind of elaborate scheme. They would have killed Nasir and left his body in the nearest room with a note: RIP you rotten bastard.

Clever. Strategic thinker. Strong enough to take a body to the morgue and hide it in the cold storage locker.

Stuck for any further insight, he remembered he had considered driving over to Ali's house to check on him, there was this gruesome image plaguing Lenny's mind of the man lying dead at home for days from a stroke before anyone discovered him.

He tried one last phone call. As he listened to Ali's voice message, again, Lenny recalled the clean, bare desk in the man's cubbyhole. Except for the computer monitor and keyboard, there was nothing else there. Not even a photograph...of a little baby girl.

"Jesus fucking Christ!"

Patience pulled the headphones off again when she heard her husband explode in a curse. "What's wrong, Lenny, what happened?"

"I just figured out who killed Boris Nasir. And why."

He went over the case with her step by step. He explained why Clair had eloped that night, where she had been hiding all this time, how Catherine had been a crucial part of the plan, and most important: what Clair was planning on doing next.

Patience got up, stepped over to her husband and kissed him on the bald spot on the back of his head. "I knew you'd solve this case, Lenny. It was just a matter of time."

"I have to get going. It's probably too late to catch her, but I have to give it a try."

"Are you going to call that Detective Williams?"

"No, not yet. I want to confirm my theory first. I want to hear it with my own ears, if that's possible. Then I'll see about calling the cops."

He threw on a jacket, kissed Patience and hurried out the door. At this time of night it would be a good twenty minutes before he got to the house in West Philadelphia, where he was sure Clair had been in hiding. He hoped he wasn't too late. He hoped there would be no more deaths.

43

Lenny parked a few doors down from Ali's house on Farragut Terrace, just off 46th street, the car facing the wrong direction, a common practice on Philly streets. As he walked back to the address, he saw his friend coming out of the house with two large bags. Ali opened the hatch of his SUV and was carefully stowing the bags tight against the back seat, suggesting there were more to come, when Lenny approached him. He saw that the van had a license plate from the state of Maine.

"It's a long way to go, isn't it?" Lenny said, pointing at the plate. "I bet you've got a full tank. Hell, I wouldn't be surprised if you carried extra gas in a metal fuel can."

Ali closed the latch and stood facing the back of the car. In the light from the street lamp he could see Lenny's face reflected in the rear window.

"I was thinking you would be coming by. I even wrote a note, I was going to tape it to the front door with your name on it."

"Another few minutes, I'd be reading the note."

Ali slowly turned around. "You always were one sharp son of a gun. You never took people at face value. You always suspected they were hiding something."

"Something good, something bad, but yeah, I'm pretty skeptical about the face that people put on for public consumption. Comes from years of steward duty defending people who don't always tell me the whole truth."

Lenny followed Ali back toward the house. His friend stood in front of the door, not opening it.

"You call the cops on me?"

"No. Not yet."

"You gonna call 'em?"

"Depends on what you and Clair have to say."

"Why do you think she—"

"Don't try to bullshit a bullshitter, Ali. I know she's inside, you don't travel with a pink suitcase. Let's go in and get this thing sorted out."

With a slow nod of agreement, Ali opened the door for Lenny and followed him in. As they entered the living room, Clair came down the stairs carrying a shoulder bag and a raincoat. Her hair was now red and cut short, pixie style. When she saw Lenny, she stopped and stared.

"He knows," Ali said.

"I know a lot, I don't know it all." Lenny pointed at a stuffed chair. "Shall we sit down and talk about it?"

Ali and Clair took their seat on the sofa. He took Clair's hand, kissed the palm and folded her fingers gently: she held his heart. He'd given it to her a long time ago.

"What do you want to know?" Ali said.

"Everything. Starting with how the two of you bonded over your daughter's death in the NICU. Clair was the baby's nurse, I'm guessing."

"I was one of them," said Clair, her voice cracking with emotion. "Ali's daughter was a really painful, tragic patient. Even for pediatric nurses who are used to children dying, this was a special case. It tore us all up."

"You gave Ali comfort. That part was fine. And since he was working nights back then, same as you, you ran into each other from time to time on the job."

"He'd come to fix a computer and we would find a quiet place to talk," said Clair, taking Ali's hand.

"And you told him about the abuse you suffered from your husband. Eventually."

"In time, yes, I told him. I think, because he'd endured so much pain, and his wife leaving him, I knew he would understand. I knew he would want to comfort me the same way I had comforted him when his daughter was dying."

"And then you got pregnant."

Lenny's remark stunned Clair, who asked him how did he know. Lenny admitted it was an educated guess. But when Lenny learned that Nasir had had a vasectomy, no doubt to prevent any of the women he took advantage of from ever filing a paternity suit, he immediately wondered how the husband would react if he learned his wife was pregnant...by some other man.

"So, you were desperate and you came up with the plan. New identities — Ali used to be a hacker, he was familiar with the dark side of the net. It wouldn't be a stretch for him to buy new birth certificates, new drivers licenses, new passports, even. You would use cryptocurrency for the purchases: no paper trail."

"We wanted to start our lives fresh," said Clair. "We wanted to leave the pain behind us. Mine, and his. I knew Boris would never leave us alone, we'd never have any peace if we stayed in Philly. He knows some really bad people, Lenny. Drug people."

"I understand how you had to get away clean. And since you'd administered blood transfusions in the NICU, you had friends in the blood bank who would give you a unit of outdated blood. Was it difficult to swallow it?"

Clair shrugged. "It wasn't as difficult as living with a malignant narcissist."

"The black stools was a nice touch," said Lenny. "Charcoal?"

Clair nodded a yes.

"And you faking Nasir's limp..." Lenny turned to Ali. "That was brilliant. Really smart move."

Now it was Ali's turn to nod his agreement. "We're planning to go far away. Some place the police would never find us. Maine is just the start. I guess now we'll never get there, will we?"

"That depends," said Lenny, his eyes as hard and unblinking as they had ever been.

"On what?" asked Ali.

"On why you killed Nasir. I don't blame you for doing it, but I need to know *exactly* how it happened."

"You won't believe me, it sounds lame," said Ali.

"Try me."

Ali looked at Clair, who offered him a small smile of encouragement.

"We never set out to kill the bastard," Ali said. "Never. That wasn't the plan. We set up the fake bleed and the disappearance in the middle of the night so people in the hospital would suspect Nasir had killed his wife."

"I get that. His reputation would be forever ruined."

"That's right," said Clair. "My disappearance would even protect vulnerable women on the night shift from his taking advantage of them."

Ali continued: "I'd gone to the office in the early morning hours, well before my shift would begin. I wanted to pack up my personal belongings but I didn't want anyone to see me."

"Like the photo of your daughter. Tonight I realized it was missing from your desk, which could only mean you were never coming back."

"Yes, that's right. I sneaked into the hospital by the same door we'd used to smuggle Clair out."

"The emergency door with the disabled alarm. An easy trick for a guy who works in IT."

"True, although I wasn't the one who turned off the alarm, that's been dead for weeks. Months, maybe."

"So you're in your office packing away your things..."

"Actually, I wasn't packing yet. When I opened the door to the office and stepped inside, I found Nasir at my desk. He was going through my papers, he'd opened the desk drawer, even though I always left it locked."

"A supervisor's prerogative. Childress breaks into my locker every couple of months."

"He stole Clair's password and read our emails. He realized we were in love. Then she eloped in preparation for us going away together. That was what got him hopped up: that any woman would leave *him* and not the other way around. It made him crazy with anger."

"Who struck the first blow."

"He did. The bastard packs a mean punch. But I've been in enough fights in my youth to know how to roll with a punch. I picked up a paper weight from my desk, and when his next punch sailed by my head, I hit him once, hard."

"Did you want to kill him?"

"Does it matter?"

"Maybe not. I just want to know it all."

"In that split second I was trying to defend myself, but mainly I was defending Clair. I was protecting her from his rotten soul. I could have called for help when he was on the floor. Called a code, maybe save him even, but I didn't."

"You got a stretcher and rolled him down to the morgue."

Ali admitted he had.

Clair put her hand on the side of his face and gently caressed him. She turned toward Lenny. "What are you going to do, Lenny? Are you going to talk to the police?"

"I can't avoid it, a detective has been dogging me for information from the get-go. I'll have to tell him something... but I don't have to tell him everthing, and I don't have to tell him tonight. I could wait a few days...a few weeks...a few years."

When the implications of Lenny's last comment sank in, Clair burst out in tears. Ali tried to thank him, but Lenny shook him off. He didn't want thanks, he had the truth, that was enough, and he had his own kind of working class justice.

"It's too bad you can't send me a postcard now and then," Lenny said, standing in the open front door.

"No, that wouldn't do," said Ali. "But I will send you a surprise once in a while. Anonymously, but I think you'll know who it's from."

They shook hands warmly, Ali fighting back tears, Lenny at peace with what he knew and what he'd done.

"It's kinda nice when the young couple rides off into the sunset and live happily ever after, don't you think?"

"Yes, it's kinda nice," said Ali.

Lenny got into his car and drove toward home. In his rearview mirror, he saw Ali locking the front door. In a few seconds they would be gone. Disappeared the way Clair had disappeared from her room on Seven South.

He started to laugh. The laugh rose into an overpowering thunder of joy. Lenny felt as if he could kiss the sky, to quote Jimi Hendrix. Or jump over the moon.

44

Stepping back into his house as quietly as possible, the children hopefully in bed and maybe even asleep, Lenny poured himself a double shot of Evan Williams, added a little ice and settled into his favorite chair. He was going to enjoy his peace and quiet and savor the moment for a while. When was the last time he'd pulled off such a sweet victory?

Patience came down to wish him good-night. He told her briefly about his meeting with Ali and Clair. She gave him a warm kiss and a hug.

"What was that for?" he asked.

"For being such a fine man. And for being *you*."

Not knowing how to respond, Lenny just grunted and wished her good-night. He returned to his drink and his reverie, enjoying the peace and quiet and wishing he could sit there undisturbed for eternity. He wondered if Ali would drive all night in order to get as much distance as he could between Philadelphia and his final destination. He guessed they were heading for Canada. New Brunswick, perhaps, or Nova Scotia. He wouldn't be surprised if they even had Canadian ID.

The smile on his face lingered for some time, until a rap-rap on the door interrupted him.

Who the hell would be coming by at this time of night?

Opening the door, Lenny was not surprised to find Detective Williams on the porch glowering at him.

"Don't you answer your phone after the sun goes down?" Williams stood there looking unhappy.

"Jesus Christ," said Lenny, glancing at his watch. "Eleven at night. Can't a body ever get some peace and quiet?"

"You gonna let me in or do I need to get a search warrant?"

With a sigh, Lenny stepped back to allow the detective into the house.

Williams pushed a bottle at Lenny's chest. "My turn to buy the drinks," he said and walked past Lenny into the living room.

"Jim Beam. Wow. Not exactly high end, but I'll drink it anyway." He went to the kitchen to fetch a glass for the detective and ice, knowing the detective didn't take a mixer. Returning, he saw that Detective Williams was not smiling.

The two men sipped their drinks and kept their own counsel. The silence wasn't threatening, as it would be in an interrogation, Lenny had questioned enough hostile witnesses to know the difference.

Finally, Williams said, "I've got it in my mind the Nasir case is going to end up in the cold case files."

"Uhmm," Lenny said.

"Was that you agreeing with me?"

"No, that was me saying 'Uhmm,'"

"The thing is, we've found no trace of Clair Bowen. We don't know if she's dead or in hiding somewhere."

"Uh-huh."

Williams glared at Lenny, unhappy with the lack of information. "Do you really expect me to believe you haven't learned *anything* new about this case? I can lock you up as a material witness. I can charge you with obstructing a police investigation. You realize that, don't you?"

"I'm just wandering in the dark, like the rest of humanity." Lenny sipped his drink, enjoying his silence and knowing how much it annoyed Williams.

Williams looked over his glass and said, "It's funny how this whole case began with a woman disappearing from her room in the hospital. I'm starting to agree, she started out faking her GI bleed to get away from her abusive husband. But you know, that still doesn't mean she got out of the place alive."

"True, true," said Lenny.

"I'm not finding this interview funny, Moss. I thought we had a better understanding. You know, I tell you something, you tell me, remember?"

Williams waited for Lenny to comment, but the wily shop steward just stared into his glass and said nothing.

"I'll tell you something, just between you and me and the wall," said Williams. "Personally, I think she had a boyfriend and the two of them sailed away to some enchanted island somewhere. I think she and the boyfriend killed Nasir along the way, although I don't have a shred of evidence to support my theory. Just my understanding of human behavior."

"That's a positive thought. It's nice to not hear a cynical one."

"If they did go off together, I hope Clair Bowen finds some kind of peace and happiness. God knows, she deserves it," said Williams.

"I agree. Putting Clair in prison for twenty years for killing an abusive husband would not exactly be justice. Not the way I look at the world."

"Does it surprise you, Lenny, that I see the case pretty much the same way?"

Lenny contemplated the detective's remarks. "Not really, no, it doesn't. You're a smart guy. You see how the system is corrupt. A rich guy who rapes young girls and procures them for his rich and powerful friends gets off with a slap on the wrist, and then goes on raping and procuring for *years* because his friends are so fucking..."

"Rich and powerful. Hey, we read the same news reports. We see the same shit year after year. How do you uphold 'the law' when the strings are pulled by greedy, sexist bastards? They put young black men away for life and let white kids from the 'burbs off with a misdemeanor and community fucking service. It bothers the hell out of me."

"You want to hear something interesting?" said Lenny, topping up his and the detective's glasses. "It's the same in my little world. In the hospital. Same corruption, same injustice." He explained how the administration was suing poor patients, attaching their benefits to discourage them from being admitted so they could attract a more upscale clientele. "Medical gentrification," he added.

Williams was disgusted, but he wasn't surprised.

Lenny went on to say that he had spent most of his adult life battling for dignity and fairness in the workplace. For living wages and a pension so workers didn't have to work until they dropped dead on the job.

But then he mentioned what his father used to tell him: that the workers and the community ought to operate the hospital for the good of the people.

"Now wouldn't that be something?" said Williams.

"I can win a battle here and win a battle there, but I'm never gonna win the war when the system is rigged by the people on top."

They spent another few minutes drinking and ruminating.

"Life sucks," Williams said.

"No, said Lenny, "It's not life that sucks, it's the damn system that sucks. It's gotta change. We have to figure out a better way."

"A better way. Yeah, I'll drink to that."

They clinked glasses and emptied them.

"One more for the road?" asked Williams.

"Might as well."

Lenny got up to retrieve more ice.

45

Lenny was in the sewing room on morning break, drinking his coffee and not dunking his donut. Birdie was working away at her big black industrial sewing machine, while Moose was sketching a drawing of his wife with charcoal. He asked Lenny if he ever thought about leaving his job and doing something else.

"What else would I do?" asked Lenny. "Clean offices in Center City? Or maybe wash windows on a scaffold thirty floors above the ground. Yeah, that would be a great career move."

"You could teach. You could get your degree. How many classes you need to finish?"

"That was years ago, Moose, I don't even know if I could get credit for them."

"That's what I'm saying: you don't know 'cause you haven't checked it out."

"Ah, I'm a hundred years away from retiring."

"I'm just looking at your future, you can't push a mop the rest of your life. The guys that sit at desks all day, their bodies hold up for the long haul, but us guys in the trenches, it wears a body out."

"Yeah, I know, I've petitioned for a disability early retirement for more than a few workers. It's a bitch getting it for them, lemme tell you."

Lenny didn't want to admit it, but he'd been feeling some aches in his knees lately, especially in cold weather. He hadn't told Patience, or Moose, but it did send a twinge of worry through his mind: What if he couldn't do the custodian work on the ward anymore? Could he tolerate working as a ward clerk? Could he give up his navy-blue uniform and black, steel-tipped shoes and come to work in a jacket and tie? It was a line of thought he tried to suppress, but sometimes the fear of becoming disabled couldn't be held down.

"I'm good for another twenty years," said Lenny. "Let's drop it."

A knock on the door. Mimi opened it and poked her head in. "Okay if I join you guys?"

"You're always welcome, Mimi, you know that," said Birdie, pointing to a battered old folding chair for her to use. The nurse settled in and watched as Moose continued his art work.

"You better not be drawing me in a caricature," Birdie said. "I got a lot of needles here at my disposal."

"Heh, heh. I draw 'em as I see 'em."

Lenny said that reminded him of an old joke his father used to tell. "Three baseball umpires were having drinks after a game. The first one says, 'I call 'em as I see 'em.' The second umpire says, 'I call 'em as they are.' The third ump says, 'You guys got it all wrong. They ain't fair *or* foul until I call 'em."

Moose groaned and complained the joke was too deep for him. Birdie agreed, she preferred Lenny's puns. That brought Lenny to recall Freddie, the old morgue attendant and his awful knock-knock jokes. He missed the old morgue fellow. Helping load an extra heavy body onto the morgue cart just wasn't the same without him.

Mimi agreed, Freddie had been a pleasure to work with. She said she was so happy that Margie won her paid parental leave, and kept her job. "I wish us nurses had a union like you guys," she said. She turned to Lenny and asked if he thought Catherine would get her job back. Lenny said it was in the hands of her lawyer now, he didn't have any way he could help her, much as he wished he could.

"So, you never discovered what happened to Clair?" Mimi asked.

"I didn't say that exactly."

"Well, what...?"

Moose stopped sketching and poked Mimi. "You know there's some things he can't talk about. Some things you have to put to rest and just let them lie."

"Then you *do* know what happened!" Mimi said.

Lenny sipped his coffee and took a bite out of his donut.

"Just tell me one thing, Lenny, just one thing. She's okay? Clair's okay?"

"Yes, Clair is okay."

"Praise god," Mimi said. "And I just know that Catherine had a hand in her eloping, but she won't say any more than you will, huh?"

Lenny admitted Catherine would rather lose her job at James Madison than betray a friend. A sister. But he wasn't ready to tell Mimi how much the night nurse had helped with the affair. "Detective Williams threatened me with all kinds of jail time if I didn't cough up everything I knew," Lenny said. "Material witness, accessory after the fact, co-conspirator. He was supremely pissed 'cause he was sure I knew what happened."

"You mean you didn't tell the police anything?" said Mimi.

Moose looked slyly at his friend, then said, "Nobody talks, everyone walks." He explained that when workers under threat kept their secrets, it was their best chance of walking away from the law. Lenny drank his coffee and kept mum.

"Well I hope Clair ended up someplace sunny," said Mimi. "Like Hawaii, that would be a sweet place to live. I can see her there swimming in the ocean, drinking a Mai tai as the sun sets over the beach, and finding somebody kind and gentle to love."

"Maybe she's there," said Moose, who resumed his drawing. The hum of the sewing machine was the only sound in the room. That, and the sound of four hospital workers' beating hearts as they celebrated the freedom of a woman abused and the man who helped her: the lovers who got away and lived happily ever after.

ACKNOWLEDGEMENTS

Words are never enough to express my debt to the friends and colleagues who helped me keep the Lenny Moss saga going. My wife Mary is number one in support. She has a keen understanding of crime stories and labor stories that helps me develop and revise my stories. Thank you, my dear.

David "Q" Bass: he is the anchor that keeps Hard Ball & Little Heroes Press from crashing on the shoals of my over weaning ambition and disorganized work habits. Thank you, Dave, I couldn't build the press without you.

Larry Christenson, thank you for acting as one of the "Beta readers" who gave me feedback and encouragement for the story. And thank you for your meticulous proof reading: every good writer needs an even better editor.

Finally, deepest, most heartfelt thanks to the readers who nag me repeatedly, saying, "When is the next Lenny Moss novel coming out?" Your enthusiasm for my characters keeps the flame of creativity burning.

ABOUT THE AUTHOR

Veteran nurse Timothy Sheard is a writer, publisher, mentor to writers and union organizer with the National Writers Union, UAW Local 1981. After writing several mystery novels featuring hospital custodian-shop steward Lenny Moss, he launched Hard Ball & Little Heroes Press to help working class people write and publish their stories. Hard Ball & Little Heroes has published the work of over 200 authors, including stories for children as well as grownups.

Timothy believes that when workers write and tell their stories, they build rank and file solidarity and union power, and they advance the fight for social justice. Their stories help to combat the anti-labor and anti-working class assaults by the One Percent, allowing the reader to walk in the worker's shoes, face the challenges, and find joy in the victories. Hard Ball Press is proud to publish books about working class life.

TITLES FROM HARD BALL PRESS

A Great Vision: A Militant Family's Journey Through the Twentieth Century, Richard March

Caring: 1199 Nursing Home Workers Tell Their Story, Tim Sheard, ed.

Fight For Your Long Day, Classroom Edition, by Alex Kudera

Good Trouble: A Shoeleather History of Nonviolent Direct Action, Steve Thornton

I Just Got Elected, Now What? A New Union Officer's Handbook, 3rd Edtion, Bill Barry

I Still Can't Fly: Confessions of a Lifelong Troublemaker, Kevin John Carroll

In Hiding – A Thriller, Timothy Sheard

Justice Is Our Love In Action: Poetry & Art for the Resistance, Steward Acuff (author), Mitch Klein (Artist)

Legacy Costs: The Story of a Factory Town, Richard Hudelson

Love Dies – A Thriller, Timothy Sheard

The Man Who Fell From the Sky – Bill Fletcher, Jr.

Murder of a Post Office Manager – A Legal Thriller, Paul Felton

My Open Heart: 1199 Nursing Home Workers Tell Their Story

New York Hustle: Pool Rooms, School Rooms and Street Corner, A Memoir, Stan Maron

The Secrets of the Snow –Poetry, Hiva Panahi

Sixteen Tons – A Novel, Kevin Corley

Throw Out the Water – Sequel to Sixteen Tons, Kevin Corley

The Union Member's Complete Guide, 2nd Edition, Updated & Revised, Michael Mauer

Welcome to the Union (pamphlet), Michael Mauer

What Did You Learn at Work Today? The Forbidden Lessons of Labor Education, Helena Worthen

Winning Richmond: How a Progressive Alliance Won City Hall – Gayle McLaughlin

With Our Loving Hands: 1199 Nursing Home Workers Tell Their Story, Timothy Sheard, ed.

Woman Missing – A Mill Town Mystery, Linda Nordquist

The Lenny Moss Mysteries (in order of release) – Timothy Sheard

This Won't Hurt A Bit

Some Cuts Never Heal

A Race Against Death

Slim To None

No Place To Be Sick

A Bitter Pill

Someone Has To Die

One Foot in the Grave

All Bleeding Stops Eventually (2020 release)

Hard ball Press Children's Books on next page

Children's & Young Adult Books

The Cabbage That Came Back, Stephen Pearl (author), Sara Pearl (translator), Rafael Pearl (Illustrator)

Freedom Soldiers, a YA novel, Katherine Williams

Good Guy Jake, Mark Torres (Author), Yana Muraskho (Illustrator), Madelin Arroyo (Transslator)

Hats Off For Gabbie!, Marivir Montebon (author), Yana Murashko (Illustrator), Laura Flores (Translotor)

Jimmy's Carwash Adventure, Victor Narro (author), Yana Murashko (Illulstrator), Madelin Arroyo (Translator)

Joelito's Big Decision, Ann Berlak (Author), Daniel Camacho (Illustrator), Jose Antonio Galloso (Translator)

Manny & the Mango Tree, Ali Bustamante (Author), Monica Lunot-Kuker (Illustrator), Mauricio Niebla (Translator)

Margarito's Forest, Andy Carter (author), Allison Havens (illustrator) Omar Majeia (translator)

Polar Bear Pete's Ice Is Melting! (A 2020 release) Timothy Sheard (author), Kayla Fils-Aime (Illustrator), Madelin Arroyo (Translator)

Trailer Park, JC Dillard (Author), Anna Usacheva (Illustrator), Madelin Arroyo (Translator)